through a glass darkly

a novel in verse

Libby Hathorn

1 Though I speak with the tongues of men and of angels, but have not love I am only a resounding gong or clanging cymbal resounding in the wind.

2 And though I have the gift of prophecy, and can understand all mysteries and all knowledge, and though I have faith, that can move mountains, but have not love, I am nothing.

3 And though I give all I possess to the poor, and surrender my body to the flames, but have not love, I gain nothing.

4 Love is kind; love does not envy; love does not parade itself, is not puffed up; 5 does not behave rudely, does not seek its own, is not provoked, thinks no evil; 6 does not rejoice in iniquity, but rejoices in the truth; 7 bears all things, believes all things, hopes all things, endures all things.

8 Love has no fear; it does not worry; love keeps no records of wrongs; never fails. But whether there are prophecies, they will fail; whether there are tongues, they will cease; whether there is knowledge, it will vanish away. 9 For we know in part and we prophesy in part. 10 But when that which is perfect has come, then that which is in part will be done away.

11 When I was a child, I spoke as a child, I understood as a child, I thought as a child; but when I became a man, I put away childish things. 12 For now we see through a glass darkly, but then face to face. Now I know in part, but then I shall know just as I also am known.

13 And now abide faith, hope, love, these three; but the greatest of these is love.

1 Corinthians 13:12
King James Version

'What in me is dark
Illumine...'
Paradise Lost. John Milton

Contents

Part 1 - The Pond

By the pond — 11

In the garden of the world — 13

Fecund — 15

Poetry bits... — 19

And Clea — 23

A jag — 26

Totti's damned song — 28

Part 2 - Kings Cross

Rob unexpected — 35

Rob of Kings Cross — 40

A betrayal — 43

Those books — 47

Black Orpheus, the Cross, and Vietnam — 51

A fortune teller — 57

Part 3 - Suburbia

Doing time in the burbs... — 63

A wedding — 65

Loves past — 71

Totti and Toby — 73

'and they're racing...' — 75

Part 4 - Writing

When she writes... — 81

Tom and marriage — 84

Rosie, his child — 86

Darlinghurst Rob — 89

Part 5 - The Blue Mountains

Suddenly Henry   95
'the pilgrim soul in you'   98
Blue, Blue Mountains and Henry   101
Wine bar   104
Max of Matra   106
Max of Taylor Square   109
Henry and friend   112
Pine forest and mountains   114

Part 6 - The Kiss

Henry on return   119
On first meeting Rob Connor   122
Her own child   126
Who are you Tom? Who am I?   130
Illicit love   135
Rilke in Rodin's house, Paris   138
Going home   141
Her mental state   145
Blue, Blue Mountains and Rob   149
Train journey away   153
Confession   156
Ecstasy   159
Making love   162
Serious stuff   167

Part 7 - Normandy, France to Sydney Again

With Tom in Normandy   173
In the ruined chateau, in the ruined marriage   176
'Today I have been happy'   182
For the love of poetry, for the love of Evie?   187
Mont Saint-Michele   189
Totti's story   193
Admission   198
Some promise   202

Main Characters

Evie, whose story unfolds sometimes uneasily by the pond, in fits and starts

Rob, who keeps re-appearing to her but always withholding something

Tom, Evie's marriage partner she still hopes by remembering, to understand

Henry, her first love who remains shining in her memory

Lucas, her illicit lover who helps her through a difficult marriage

Totti and Toby, fond aunt and uncle, who unfailingly help through depression, the worst of times, and encourage her towards the best.

Part 1
The Pond

'could watch life going on, without fear'

By the pond

It happened that she sat by the pond,
Out front, every day,
and they let her,
sometimes for hours on end
day after day.
Evie said she was happy there
in the overgrown garden
could watch life going on
without fear she told them
 and hear a kind of language.

'Pond-ese,' she joked
for the pond talked to her.
And they liked to laugh
the old rels, Totti and Toby,
aunt and uncle
the only rels now.
Mostly unquestioning too,
letting her stay and stay
in their sprawling house
with its generous verandahs
and slouching gardens,
its slip-shod domesticity.
Her home now, they told her,
and would really be hers, one day,
their only surviving niece.
With a room of her own
with her books and a desk,
with her art pieces and

clumsy folders of photos
and those bundles of old letters,
and the more unremarkable trivia
that makes up a life.
There was some sort of triumph
she thought in being able to say
at the door of her room,
when she rejoined them each evening,
This is my life, and it being true,
 all she needed now?

In the garden of the world

Totti, her aunt, once called this overgrown place
out here by the oval shaped pond,
the garden of the world.
'It's all here Evie,' the old aunt said simply.
And for the moment,
longer and longer moments
it seemed it was, it is?

A hovering dragon fly, a hornet darting by
or even the not-green small frogs,
the dirty-looking little slithery amphibians
that at night left so much spawn.

Spawn a funny wet word you could
draw out and out - spaaaawn.
She baulked. No, don't go there...
One of those dynamite words.

Or a moth careering, on lucky days
a butterfly, the orange and black variety.
Ah, the Monarch! she remembered gratefully
with its bold black markings,
unnecessary frilled edges.
Is there a fluttering noise, making language?
And aren't butterflies deaf?
Pretty fluttering things...
even the spiders with their
gorgeous overwhelming webs and

particularly, the dark water spoke to her,
clumped, with tilting water plants
sometime thickened by algae
but best when cleared by Toby
with the big blue-poled sieve
that took the slime and the matt
and some of the finer floating plants
and left only the struggling water lilies bobbing,
the tall reeds bunched over there,
and the fine lace-like weed in between.

Then she could easily look and look
into the dark water deep
rippling slightly now and then
announcing a tadpole or a zephyr.
Or into the stillness, a pond
that could carry the sky
at midday in full sun,
even clouds, alternately dark, then blue.
Fecund - she felt fecund there
even now. And why that word?
It was the Rob Connor word.

Fecund

He'd called her that, one evening
long ago. Fecund. Rob Connor had.
After college she'd meet him,
flying through Sydney city streets
with her student bags over her shoulder
her duffle coat flying open
to coffee shops in the trendy Rowe Street
or to some more fabulous venue
he always stage managed for her,
'being impecunious' as he explained,
but not without imagination. Never!

Once it had been the grand chandelier-lit foyer,
the State Theatre with its sweeping double staircase,
its marble pillars and columns, flamboyant with marble insets.
Marble, marble, its luxury spread everywhere,
white, green, brindle, with the tile-studded floor.
And he welcomed her, she who'd rushed from the bus
over eager, as if into his own place, a place perhaps
into his heart as he'd once dramatically declaimed.

The cloying theatre smell,
the burring words and intermittent music
floating from that plush interior curtained place.
And just the two of them out here, foyered.
Purply velvet chairs tempting with their golden arms,
his soft grey male-smelling coat,
his old leather briefcase slung on the seat.

He told her he treasured this briefcase
handsome in its leathery way
despite being scuffed and worn.
And when she'd asked, 'your father's?'
He'd laughed and shook his head 'God no!
Someone much more important.'
And that was all. Rob Connor
right here lounging, she sitting close beside him.

Rob Connor.
His kisses and his poetry.
Why think of him here. And now?
There was an undercurrent of uneasiness
in it and she was not sure why?
Was he part of her tangled so called problem,
those unheralded times of panic?
Of the depression and unreasonableness?
But no, there he was in dark water
Rob Connor, persisting, and she succumbed.

How is it she wondered that some people
recur in your life, a man you couldn't call
a boyfriend exactly, but a close sometime friend?
A quixotic boyfriend then, a brief one.
It seems on reflection somehow,
his random appearances in her life
like scattered chapters of an incomplete novel
(and she had many such manuscripts in her desk)
 intermittent as it was, perhaps in some way
rounding off a story, her story, a little each time?
Why now?

Unimportant, in the scheme of things
yet vividly unimportant.
'This unimportant morning'
like the Durrell poem they'd loved
so much, not knowing quite why
and read out to each other
both thinking Greek isles and romance.
This unimportant morning
Something goes singing where
The capes turn over on their sides
And the warm Adriatic rides
Her blue and sun washing
At the edge of the world and its brilliant cliffs
Some poems resonate for you,
are embedded so that the lines
exact a meaning more than the words-
a special time, your childhood, your youth,
all that aching, pleasant/unpleasant longing,
whose words seal something in your mind forever.
They had read these lines to one another
and the title always thrilled her as if with them,
the unimportant had found a certain grace.

Something of those enticing discussions-
they'd had brief hours together, always of intensity,
when she felt as if they, too, were characters,
part of a larger story, happening, on the edge of happening.
Durrell and The Alexandrian Quartet
(possibly in the Sydney CBD) or
a Russian novel, or a Chekhov play
or a David Malouf novel, or a Judith Wright poem

the mysteriousness of life, of inner life.
This Rob Connor, this unimportant man
when you add it all up, in the scheme of things,
in the decades of her life since Rob Connor,
seemingly unimportant.

And yet their uneven bright story, one that
is recurring, here, right now.
Their short eventful relationship pulsates
again by the almost silent pond.
where she can clearly see more midday reflections,
the underside of several leaning palms
the ribboned fronds distinct against the sky,
and the edge of herself, head bowed over,
searching the meanings in water's reflection
she knew were almost there and real,
almost within her grasp.
The unimportant one.
The man who passes through your life
and yet does not.

Poetry bits…

'Fecund,' he'd said and it had thrilled her.
Even the night when blood flowed from her
so freely with its gushes and clots,
she knew she should change the sanitary pad
but was too ashamed to talk of such things.
to someone so out of her world,
out of this world, Rob Connor.

Fecund. The night he used that word first
they'd scampered through Darlinghurst,
'If you buy us coffees, darling one,' and then
 his friend nearby would love to see them,
 an old friend in an old Deco-style block of flats.

And yet there was only hollow sound
of an empty room when he knocked.
But halfway down the gloomy hall
a darkly moire-covered lounge presented
with its squeaky sagging springs
and there they sat in the near dark
and he kissed her again and again
and told her she was fecund.
And the blood flowed from her
even more freely with the desire,
for him this dark-haired, dark-eyed man
who looked like a languid Oscar Wilde
with his long loose body and dandyish clothes,
his flamboyant often tender language. Fecund

She thought her blood might stain the lounge
but could not move. Fecund.
She would double check its meaning at home,
but it sounded good and strong, sexual.

And of how it had seemed
that the end of that sporadic
strung out relationship came too swiftly.
How eventually he'd told her gently
taking her by the hand as they walked
through a grand arch of trees turning
into the sunken garden of Hyde Park,
'I've something to say to you, Little Evie,'
and how her heart sank even then,
to sit atop the semi-circle of stone stairs
where they'd come often
(their private garden he called it)
over the uncertain months,
to talk and test each other's recitations,
classic poems they'd made a challenge to learn
by heart. Very much by heart for her.

The Romantics, of course the Romantics
but more often than not, just John Keats.
'So sensuous to say aloud,' as Rob Connor
opined leaning back on the shallow steps
and between long puffs, long exhalations
of his sleek Sobrani cigarettes,
reciting the first verse word perfect.
Now you must learn his Ode to Autumn
my favourite he'd said in that first visit

and she'd committed most of it to memory
so that she could recite it even now
out loud if she wished, to the pond.
 Season of mists and mellow fruitfulness,
 Close bosom-friend of the maturing sun;
 Conspiring with him how to load and bless
 With fruit the vines that round the thatch-eves run;
 To bend with apples the moss'd cottage-trees,
 And fill all fruit with ripeness to the core.

In a change of mood one afternoon
a sadder poem, the death of his brother
Rob told her, 'No, not mine, Don't have one!
John Keats brother Tom.'
He caught the TB bug from Tom too,
the one that killed him. Consumption
they called it then and sent the sufferer
to seek the sun, sometimes worked
but for him the young Keats, didn't.
'Twenty five years old! The waste!'
As if John Keats a dear friend to him,
and it probably was true for him
 as Keats sometimes seemed to her.

'So let's commit to him!' he challenged.
And they took whole verses
Sometimes even whole poems to heart.
My heart aches and a drowsy numbness pains my senses
As though of hemlock I had drunk
Or emptied some dull opiate to the drains
A minute past and Lethe-wards had sunk:

Darkling I listen; and, for many a time
    I have been half in love with easeful Death,
Call'd him soft names in many a mused rhyme,
    To take into the air my quiet breath.

She'd learnt it as easily as he
and they could oblige each other
by the quiet shining pond, his lounging figure
on sprawling steps ever more appealing,
the shock of dark hair, brown eyes
and sensuous mouth, smiling mouth
with their recitations, too.

And Clea

One afternoon, he'd told her gently
carefully choosing that place,
their verdant outdoor room
to be splendidly memorable.
Down those familiar shallow steps
tiered gardens defiantly in bloom
to the shallow tiled pond
with its occasional water show.
'Memorial made for some English king or other,'
he'd said. 'Died before he got here,
to Australia that is, so they made it a garden.
For us!'

Walking close enough to feel
the brush of his coat,
the warmth of the hand holding hers
they went to view
the sunken garden once again,
Hyde Park but not, she thought,
Rather today a nowhere a place
where every word spoken
shaped the future, and silences delayed it.
She pulled away from him
and she walked for a moment indulgently
apart from him
inspecting the pond, then
looking back and up
at the wisteria coming into bloom.

He came and took her arm then and she sat beside him
feeling strangely cold on the hard stone step.
All these long months together...
He'd told her that he'd been seeing
 a grownup woman. 'You remember Clea...'
Yes, she remembered fascinating friendly Clea
who'd fled her own past, changed her name from Carol,
had daringly taken a flat at the Cross.
Kings Cross the exotic, the frightening, the beguiling
with its oh so European appeal,
as European as you could get anywhere in Australia.
Parties in Clea's Kings Cross flat,
dancing, hours of dancing, sweet white wine
in cardboard containers at vantage points
then subsiding, late night their heads on cushions
desultory talking, smoking and watching the drift
Clever pretty Clea, of the nearby stone-faced library
with its imposing edifice, and important librarians.
Clea, willowy and ten years older. Grown up.
Proper job, proper flat of her own,
a woman he'd said of her that hard afternoon
as if that signified Clea's supreme suitability
and her own impossible girlishness,
not something she could perfect for some years
no matter how she might try...

Would live with her in her flat at King Cross
right near the posh Chelsea Restaurant,
Macleay St Evie, the street with
bitter green leaved trees and another fountain
they'd sat by some evenings, pretending Paris
And it'd be best if... in that sunken garden

the loggia effortlessly overgrown
flamboyant with trailing vines that at this moment
seemed somehow to intrude,
'be best,' said so wisely, holding her hands in his,
she should be with students, folk her own age,
and even then in the pain that seared
as her heart sank too
she heard there was relief in his voice.
'I'll be living with Clea you see.
Moving in with Clea.' Clea the woman.
For in all this time, he only stayed with friends.
'Temporarily, without house you see...
temporarily impecunious, my darling.'

That night on the bus home she realised
he'd had no home perhaps for months now,
Rob Connor, the fascinating,
the talented, the loquacious,
His friend Reece had explained to her,
 an enigmatic man from Adelaide, here to work
in the glamorous world of 'advertising,'
who works only spasmodically, his word.
She realised with surprise, strictly speaking
you could call Rob Connor homeless
until the beneficence of Clea.

But it wasn't over, not really
There'd be bursts of Rob Connor,
emanations, gusts and surges of Rob Connor
threading through her life,
always that shadowy link,
like now at the pond.

A jag

And why on earth was she still in this jag,
the Rob O'Connor jag?
It wasn't exactly first love
or a full-blown relationship
on and then off and then in between
months and months
over a long straggling year.
But it had elements of that first madness of love
the utter romance of it,
and it was clear to her
she needed to rethink him
the something else about him
and its impact on her life?
Something not so easy...

The shrink had said it didn't hurt
to turn things over in your mind
but it was dangerous if she thought too much,
if she let some things escape her,
as if a maleficence lurked not with him
and memories of him
though he had insinuated some
terrible revelation time to time,
not with him, Rob Connor
but with her, inside her,
something inescapable.
She pushed the thought into the pond
under that fat water lily leaf, deep,

and trailed her fingers
in a good cold,
the language of the pond
sunk deep again.

Totti's damned song

They'd be calling her in soon, the olds.
The sun well passed mid-sky
and it was a coolness coming, reminding her
to leave but this place, the pond
was still talking...
and so the garden too
and that spider she needed to watch
and write

    The silence is steaming,
    pecked into by a bird call,
    torn at by a far off traffic thrum
    Above, my 8-legged
    not-so-friend is busy weaving,
    threads glinting, alluring
    in the sunshine's drama,
    a perfect pattern of becoming...
    How many will blunder into
    your airy stranded cage
    ugly beauty?
    My own so busy, death-trap spider?
    holding me here to wonder
    What's my big life, to do with yours
    in the garden so abundant?

So many times listening
to the profound, herbaceous Totti,
'Gardening lovey, you never tire of it!'
Totti bent over some myriad flower garden bed,

eyes bright from under her
droopy, horribly old tennis hat.
'Something new every day, love.
Something huge every season,
Something soothing in digging, love,'
with spades full of dirt flying,
her plump arms so powerful.

'And the surprises on and on,' she puffed
'The first time you see the new packets of bulbs
in the garden shop and you know
that a whole year has gone around again.
All those hyacinths and snow drops
my favourites though, the old daffodils
"struggling up" out of the dark
of a whole year towards the light.'

As she talks huffs and puffs
Dylan Thomas words surface among the flower beds
among her own mysterious lines recurring like mantra

> 'The force that through the green fuse drives the flower
> Drives my green age; that blasts the roots of trees
> Is my destroyer.'

'Dug through a few sorrows of my own, love,' Totti confided.
And Evie knew her aunt was referring to her lost babies.
'Gardening' she paused to straightening her back
'It's- it's- 'as she reached for the word- 'good!'
'It's *grounding,* ha ha!' quite pleased by it.
'Dirt under your nails and roots round your fingers
digging and digging.' (and the sorrow more manageable)
she didn't mention her sorrow, but Evie knew.

Toby had told her one afternoon
when Totti was still outside gardening,
and he could hear her 'singing that damned song,'
as her husband Toby referred to it.
The first time she'd heard him annoyed and
she craned to listen some old-fashioned thing
about love, something about 'fish gotta swim, birds gotta fly'
Totti singing in her almost tuneless voice.
'I gotta love one man till I die,'
And Evie understood from some dark concern
it wasn't Toby she was referring to…
'Her damned spoilt rotten brother,' he muttered.
Evie dimly remembered him, Sam wasn't it?
and that he'd died. But Totti never mentioned him,
even though she'd more than once mentioned the babies.

One afternoon at her sewing machine
where she was making Evie a skirt
in some soft but strident Indonesian batik
Evie had found at a market years ago,
unfolding the so black, so brown flowery thing,
and loving it all over again,
Totti suddenly announcing
'I made a lot of baby clothes you know!'
Oh?
'Twice I was expecting, lovey, twice I miscarried
and then no more.' A silence.
'This will suit you – just lovely!'
said through the pins held capably
at the corner of her mouth,
her kind eyes glittering.

Totti didn't often dwell on sad things.
'Don't say anything, lovey,' Toby had said,
'About her brother Sam. Dead now 15 years!'
Fetching his canary Jack out of the birdcage,
he smiled at Evie. Then adored the small bird.
'Smart little fellah, eh?'

Part 2
Kings Cross

'wine bars and bohemians, a sense of adventuring'

Rob unexpected

What about the dream-like night
the sky upside down in the harbour, walking,
on her way from Circular Quay to the bus home.
Watching the water, slicks of oil coiling like magic things,
ferries chugging in, butting the wharf,
the moon at large.
She was swooped up into another life again
His. Rob Connor's as if he'd fallen from heaven-
Well - driven from there
in a small but fancy sports number,
more than a year later at least, not his own car.
Calling her across the pavement,
jumping from the car an irresistible jack-in-the-box,
in a dark suit, coat flying,
'Hey Evie! It *is* you! Come with us! You must!'
indicating the young man whose car it was
half in love with Rob, that was plain.
It seemed she walked through stars
towards his outstretched arms
Rob Connor. Rob!

Across the shining harbour bridge
under the great steel arch
'to meet my fiancée Cressy,' he said.
'I want you to meet her, '
 as if they'd been in constant contact.
 Clea's name was on her lips,
her Kings Cross flat, her nights

of such deeply satisfying conversations
figures in the half dark, so much talking, so close to Rob
Clea's frequent languorous embraces of Rob
with more wine, more cigarettes, embraces
from which she'd had to turn away,
heart's contraction,
talking fervently to Reece or whomsoever.

But she let Rob sweep her up in his fervour
for his new love Cressida. 'Still studying at the Con.
So musical and I want Carl to meet her.
Carl here is a pianist and I'm going to
show him off. Need to impress the olds you see
Desperate to impress!'

Some stiffly opulent house, deeply on the north shore.
A smotheringly neat garden, yet open-hearted camellias
crowding them at the doorway,
not-so-welcoming parents and a grand piano,
theatrical white against dark swooping curtains,
the glowering father, the nervous mother
and bride to be, his sweet Cressida.

In her room Cressy proudly showed her
the books Rob had bestowed on her.
Seated on the floor the girl took them
one by one lovingly from the bookshelf,
her upturned face so admiring as she gave
them into Evie's hands. Precious things,
her young face smiling but serious.
Poetry, philosophy, and she recognised
the same inscription on one title page

To my dearest darling. Because...
She had not quite relinquished
that same small book he'd given her
with the self same inscription.
It was pretty with its leafy borders
and his artistic scrawl across the fly leaf
the haiku poems, some thirty of them.
She had found them desperately modern
and mostly disappointing,
as she found most modern haiku
though she could never tell him that.
It had made her turn back to the masters
to Basho and Issa and Buson
to reassure herself of the Japanese wonder.

Above Cressy's bent head Rob smiled at her
and she was complicit, smiling back
both like relieved parents somehow,
her heart contracting, even hoping for him
with this new child-bride.
Maybe she, Evie, was the 'woman' now,
 almost two years on.

Carl played Grieg's *Piano Concerto in A*
(Where does he find these people?)
No Arthur Rubinstein but passages of brilliance,
impressive deft fingering, generous with emotion
so generous at first she thought she could love Carl to death.
That sparkling night, Carl swooping and working so hard
over those showy notes at the wrongly white baby grand
and the parents unfreezing in their chintzy armchairs
sipping their wine, nodding occasionally

almost smiling, exchanging pertinent glances.
And then somehow she wanted to spoil it for them,
smile at Rob and say loudly, 'I prefer Rachmaninoff
or the Emperor. Or Chopin's far more subtle...'
Later over supper wishing for Carl herself,
she watched the parents quiz him,
a part happy musical quiz
ignoring Rob, ignoring her,
turning an accusing eye on Cressy,
time to time, lost in Rob's loving gaze.

She doesn't remember much of the homeward journey.
Maybe it was under the returning arch of the bridge
she came out of the enchantment
the summery night, the slight madness
of a starry kind of escapade,
Cressy's adoring-ness,
Carl's music splendid and resounding
on the stagey baby grand,
the brief account of Clea's unreasonable demands of him...

His Macleay Street sojourn with Clea.
'All this business about dirty plates
and the washing if you please! Let alone the groceries.
And cursing me when I tried to read in peace and quiet,
and it was philosophy for God's sake, Evie darling,
a Spinoza craze!' his more than an adequate excuse.
'Actually told me to leave in the end, she did,
tears and all, and I was more than willing, pet.
Just couldn't take any more, her working class anxieties.'
Rob added sadly that her sense of adventure completely gone,
you wouldn't have recognised her. 'No more parties.

Her anger, her fucking domesticity, oh you know...'
Evie didn't know. And she didn't want to know anymore,
but an image of Clea persisted a while, she couldn't shrug away,
the beneficence of Clea, her lovely eyes, those heartfelt embraces
and *Grieg's Piano Concerto* somehow backgrounding it.

Clea somewhere crying. She shook her head.
Yet being with Rob, in his aura
some always magic for her about the man.
Leaning against his heartbeat
to say goodnight, the rather too long kiss,
the ineffable sadness.

Rob of Kings Cross

Liaisons, how many in a lifetime?
Shaping a lifetime or
measuring out your life, not in coffee spoons,
(hmm more teaspoons in her world)
so much as in lovers and liaisons.
And Rob Connor. What of him?
What was the dark past in Adelaide
or somewhere else, hinted at
she struggled to remember?
Did it matter?
What was it she was trying to remember
about him, to resurrect to interrogate?
A remittance man, a criminal, a bounder?
as one of her aunts had described
one of her own cheating husbands so often.
'The rotten bounder!' after another of his misadventures
 related to an admiring, ever-judgemental group.

Anyway, Kings Cross as home-ground
so right for Rob Connor.
He who could not be trapped in the suburbs,
as she was. Evie could not begin to imagine him
and daily life there. Rob Connor off to work,
leaving a semi-detached cottage in the burbs
with its too low brick fence,
his long legs would easily step over.
Carrying his impressive old briefcase
and avoiding prams and lawn mowers,

looping straddling hoses and small talk.
Could not.

No, better to think of him free-floating at the Cross
a magnet, an always enticing place.
less frightening with time
but dangerous nevertheless.
She had liked discovering its exotic offerings
never strolling but walking
with that edge of anxiety in her footsteps
along crowded footpaths,
but only an edge. She was 19 then and
there was so much to find and find out!

Shops called coffee shops! Indian jewellery for sale.
A late night bookshop, unheard of in Sydney till this one,
with teetering piles of books. No A&R or Dymocks this.
Books from other worlds. Poetry in translation.
That there were such things. Yes, Japanese haiku from
the masters. Ah yes, Basho, Issa and Shiki,
and Lorca in Spanish and in translation, Baudelaire.
Translations of everyone, everything!
The teeming world at hand!
And you could sit on the floor if you could find a space
and read from any of them if you had no money to buy...

 Wine bars and bohemians.
A sense of adventuring, but aware somehow
always aware of the sleaziness too,
dark repellent things not too far distant,
fights and brawls and sprawling figures
addictions and desperation. Fear. Sadness.

The sad dark world, away from the light,
the full-on sordid part, a frenetic nightlife,
one she didn't want to know.

Walked quickly by the plethora
of Adult Only shops in Darlinghurst Road,
ever a spruiker at the door,
a steep stark stairway leading up,
the knowing wink if you caught his eye.
'Come on up, girly!
never know what you might find up here.'

A betrayal

She'd gone up similar narrow stairs once
at the Cross. Somewhere near here,
Before Rob, before Henry,
Surrey Street or Barcom Avenue
perhaps. A stranger on a bus,
travelling along Elizabeth St
just passed the Great Synagogue
by leafy Hyde Park, rolling and jolting
towards David Jones the St James
and then Martin Place.
And her newish boyfriend, her waiting friend.
A polite hand on her shoulder
noticing his clipped English accent
as he commented on the book she was reading
and how he just loved D.H. Lawrence, too.
Someone was waiting for her at Martin Place
right now and she should go on,
and not get off with him at William Street.
Someone with fresh flowers
left waiting for her in Martin Place.
Charles with a bunch of violets in hand.
But intrigued by the stranger's constant patter
she'd allowed it!
'I can't stay long…' a weak capitulation.
But permitting herself to be led up
the long wide way of William Street
headed up with its grandiose Coca Cola sign,
flashy and beckoning, straight into the heart of it

with Lawrence and R.D. Fitzgerald on his lips,
and no thoughts for Charles, not many anyway,
waiting she knew exactly where in Martin Place
the tight posy ready in his hand
as it had been these last few weeks.
Those plump little bunches
of deep purple petals shown off resoundingly
encircled with fat deep green leaves
and the vague earthy scent of them
a smell of grass and winter. Violets.

Charles by one of the flower barrows
in Martin Place sheltering out of the wind,
waiting violets in hand.
waiting and worrying...
checking his watch and the tower clock
and finally shrugging and walking off,
like some part in a musical.
She would only think of that later
shaken and ashamed,
lying to him about her delay.

Excited, only half guilty,
intrigued by this sophisticated man,
his fervid love of literature,
his playful touching of her cheek,
stopping to look into her eyes.
Then talking Judith Wright and Dylan Thomas,
towards the rooming houses
with their dark spindly staircases.
'Go ahead!' The surprise

at the smell and the dark narrowness,
and his voice somehow charged, impatient now.
'Here we are.'
The shock of a tiny dirty room, the grimy window
looking out onto a shadowy brick wall,
at other small windows set in black brick.
The realisation a lumpy double bed
dominated the small space.
A sink and a stove crammed in the corner.
Mouldy walls, no pictures,
hardly a book in sight let alone a bookcase.
The small littered table,
half eaten meals and spilling packets,
newspapers with names like 'The Truth'.
His face full on. Why hadn't she realised.
He looked older she thought, rather weasel-like?
Who was this? And where was she?

'Sit down!' and slowly, carefully
 taking one of the cold metal chairs
and sitting straight-backed, virginal,
too frightened now to look around
any further, rigid, a panic setting in.
And he could see it.
'Relax!' and she forced a smile.
She faced the door,
the only door, the back of which
sported surely his entire wardrobe,
so much bulge that as yet,
she could not discern the door handle.
Gerald poured too much red wine

into thick waisted tumblers.
thick glasses from pubs
the ones they called something funny
not a schooner, no, they called that glass a Pony!
For some reason, she remembered
that inexplicable name, as if it mattered.
'Drink up!' his voice seemed to deepen
as he leaned towards her.
'Drink up!' His lips seemed ginger too.
There was an edge now and she knew
 it was not an invitation. 'Drink it!'
Good God she could still remember his name.
Gerald.
And how even in the dim light,
taking the sour wine,
as she considered her escape,
she saw all Gerald's shabbiness
and recognised her own.

Those books

Books, she liked to think about them.
Books made you she thought
as did a lack of books!
That's what the small precious
bookshelf, pride of place
in the lounge room of her childhood did
added to lovingly as it was by her family,
helped make you...
and later the constant search through bookshops
and that other search though library shelves.
Private 'home' libraries too, where you paid
like the one that was conveniently
near her home with the unlikely name
of the Quandong Library - amusing name,
later finding out the quandong
was a fruit favoured by Aboriginal people.
Quandongs with their bittersweet taste
and their reddish flesh, called bush peaches.
As a child she liked the beat of the word
'Quandong,' but no one could ever find one to show her.

To borrow a book then was a privilege
you must pay for, one book at a time.
And then finding the public library
a bus ride away from home,
where you could be more wanton
take out three, four at a time, no charge.
Four books read in a week with ease.

The bookcase at home had pride of place
in the lounge room near the tapestry lounge,
the good vase, Venetian glass, atop.
She remembered spines of books even now,
their order, their groupings,
of its five wide shelves specially spaced
for the bigger tomes at the base
and even a few paperbacks finding their way into the
mostly bound library of her parents' books.

Some forbidden books easily purloined
From Here to Eternity, *Sinuhe the Egyptian*
and a forensics book with the picture
of a dead man's face.
Funny what horror such an image brought
in days before television made it
more commonplace, less shocking.
And an assortment of poetry books,
The Rubaiyat of Omar Khayyam
The astronomer poet of Persia
The Fitzgerald translation,
Palgrave's *Golden Treasury of English Verse*,
a few more treasuries whatever they were,
a single book of Love Poems,
and more of Australian bush ballads.
Lots of Lawson and Kendall
and Patterson and John O'Brien
The refrain still echoing
'We'll all be rooned said Hanrahan...
Before the year is out!'
And the way they all laughed every time
though fully apprised of the ending,

because they all knew a Hanrahan
as they all knew an Eeyore.
Poor Man's Orange, her mother's favourite.
Books of knowledge eagerly fingered
What about *The Living Thoughts Library*?
Her father bought the whole set,
Thomas Mann presenting Schopenhauer
Julian Huxley presenting Darwin,
and the one she had on her own shelf now,
the only one she'd managed to keep
Theodore Dreiser presenting Thoreau.
She wondered how her father
probed their thoughts.
Just why both her parents revered books
being cheated mostly of their own education.
How her mother could quote so readily
from her precious copy of *Rubaiyat of Omar Khayam*

The Moving Finger writes;
And, having writ
Moves on: nor all they Piety
nor Wit
Shall lure it back to cancel
half a Line,
Nor all they Tears wash out
A Word of it.

Books of knowledge, with their
small black and white photos of
pyramids and temples and domed cities
to amaze and assure her of their existence,
And bible stories with coloured pictures

Daniel in the Lions' Den and
a dependable red-haired God leaning out of heaven,
with golden clouds reddish tinged and fire all round.
Books cherished, read and then displayed,
like family assets, for all to see, a treasure trove.
Hmmm a treasury. In those times
only a birthday or Christmas, or visiting aunt
provided you with a book of your own.
A book to be examined, treasured
from the fabric cover with its inky images,
to the few special plates, sometimes in colour,
to the pale cream thick paper holding its riches
by way of plot and character and time out, elsewhere.

How they were cherished! Shared with the special few,
prized and re-read for their scarcity and pleasure.
Could it have been in her lifetime such a proliferation of books?
their paper, their printing, their cheapness,
the city, the country now a vending machine
of books and more books!
The proliferation of everything!

Black Orpheus, the Cross, and Vietnam

Why was Rob dominating still? Yes,
sitting there by the pond, she allowed it,
black-edged though it seemed,
enticing nevertheless.

She had been with Rob to Kings Cross,
before his liaison with Clea.
several times to sit in coffee shops
or the Piccolo Bar, once to the movies
This time to sit inside the theatre.
Black Orpheus was playing and he mustn't miss it!
Portuguese movie set in the favelas
made only a few years ago...
and the story of Orpheus and Euridice.
'You'll just love it Evie and-
Dammit out of change!' and 'would you get the tickets, sweety?'
And Reece would join them and maybe Clea.
No, she should put thoughts of him away.
The Cross, an early taste of the exotic.
The movie and his arm carelessly slung
around her shoulders, those striking images
Black Orpheus the ancient story re-set,
The haunting music that had stayed with her,
lifted her out of suburbia so readily.

Her own place in it.
Out of the sameness of treeless suburbs,

hers with tiny white 'toy roads' as she called them
lined by lookalike semi-detached houses
and sandy grass verges with poison oleanders
and neighbours who felt it their right
to quiz her at the tram stop, to know her life,
reduce 'yours to theirs'...

King Cross at Darlinghurst where you were unknown,
streets of sleaziness outdone for her, by tree-lined ones
with handsome buildings, with continental shops
that sold coffee from large silver-handled apparatus
and spicy foods, not devon or fritz
but salamis and pickles, sauerkraut and strudels.
Despite her meagre student grant,
her first experience of schnitzels and goulash,
coffees with foreign sounding names
like cappuccino and piccolo and caffe ristretto
saying the names out loud in best Italian,
fulfilling in small ways, the longing for Europe
The place of dreams...
Fortunes won and fortunes lost here,
and fortunes told.

Coffee and wine with girl friends,
The Troubador, even the name so bohemian
folk singers like Helen Reddy far away but our own
Marion Henderson to be heard live.
Folk singers. And at the Ironworkers Hall
so daring because communists hung out there!
Lorinzini's, the first of Sydney's bistros.
She heard there were libertarians,
feminists and other 'troublemakers'
so had to go herself. Always with a friend.

Cheap drinks, a carafe of red
you could sit over for an evening,
on the edge of everything.
Nearby the national broadcasting actors
and workers meant spirited gatherings
pseudo-intellectuals and real ones
trying to make some sense
of your own innocence, naivety
your own pathetic guilelessness.
She tried to learn to smoke.

Evie supposed she was a thrill-seeker of sorts
like so many tourists, many from just across the city,
but she was a cautious, namby-pamby one.
Her artist friend Jane had helped, introducing her
To brave Jenny a new young artist from Queensland
daring enough to face the Cross,
who'd taken a room in an old hotel
a dark, interesting hotel in the centre of Kings Cross
a room with open verandahhs.
'Such a plus!' Jenny had told them,
and a glittery Bourbon and Beef Steak right under,
the signs of Americanisation coming their way,
Those loud smiling Yankee marines
with their crew cuts and their money,
the shameful acknowledgement
of our too eager part in the Vietnam War mess!

She was more taken with her new friend's
boldness, and her present room that day
than any talk of a war tonight, so close by,
though papers carried details of protests

and friends exhorted her to attend rallies.
She was admiring of Jenny
the young artist being here in the midst of it
without a sister, a mother, without a friend.
And annoyed at her own timidity,
actually being here, helped suppress it.

But it wore into her the unspeakable war
the television making it inescapable.
Bombing and defoliation more than words,
Proliferation, draft dodgers, protest,
battles and death and the poetry began,
as the photographs, the photographs
made it inescapable,
Realties, horrific, a country not so far
from her own ordered Australian life.
The one about the Australian headquarters
And the black and white photograph
of two young people etched in her mind
to the poem she'd offered to the FAW magazine
and seen it then in Vietnamese translation.

The young woman
Being led away for interrogation
with her heart-shaped face
and sweep of dark hair
looks like an old school friend.

What would they do to her?
How would they make her
captive as she was in that place
that is her country,

Not tonight that graceless direction
not today by the pond.
More about Jenny, wondering about her
being so daringly in her Kings Cross room.
Already an independent girl? Woman?
Evie remembered the wonder of that,
the very room.
Long windows with generous ledges
and solid darkish furniture,
with its wide double bed where,
first meeting upstairs,

the three young women lying together to talk,
there being no chairs,
about futures and fortune telling.
Jenny warned them both, friend Jane and her
of the Italian boys from downstairs
who might try something on.
And she remembered lying there in some discomfort
her innocence seeming quite a drawback,
her new friend seeming so sophisticated,
her old friend more at ease.
But only Gino of the bright face and brighter teeth
popped in and out and smiling at them, harmlessly,
before Jenny took them to the fortune teller.
So knowing and grownup. And to her, so brave,
to be in the centre of Kings Cross amid it all!
So young to be choosing to stay there, live there...

A fortune teller

Could a fortune teller really have the name of Probert?
A wizened man, predictably at the top of narrow
steep staircase, and not far distant from the famous
so-called witch of the Cross, Rosaleen Norton
and the poet of repute, Mary Gilmore.
How different all this was. Cosmopolitan.

Her fortune was favourably told by Mr Probert.
as if he could predict the wavering future
of any of them, but did with authority.
Fame hung in the air most pleasant
in her particular reading
and she luxuriated in words like
due recognition
'Life ahead full of good fortune' as if life itself would
naturally come and sweep her that way,
to this early recognition of her art,
and so to good fortune,
as if there was an endless stream
of days to come that would take her
in their sway and likely reward her.
Laughing their way down the narrow staircase
spilling the wisdom Probert had imparted
with mollifying suspicion,
but half believing it too.
Why do some incidents among thousands
stand out in memory?
What a strange animal the memory,
the black box so to speak.

Up another clattery staircase led by Jenny
followed by Jane,
telling the figure slouched on guard at the doorway,
'Emmanuel's a friend of mine, said I could bring
whoever I liked. No truly!'
Jenny was always laughing, explaining,
and hurrying, always meeting someone or other,
Sydney only the beginning of her escape.

'It's a party at Emmanuel's, Surry Hills,
and you better both come along.'
Climbing the narrow staircase,
two men in jeans and black t-shirts, heavy boots,
exchanging, to Evie's amazement, a deep and passionate kiss,
not moving aside as the three scrabbled past.
Up more wooden steps, their own suede boots
making too much noise on bare boards,
through a subdued hallway
to the dim lit room, swaying figures
and raucous bursts of music.
Large canvasses lending their slashes of colour,
Emmanuel's unhung works leaning all round the flat
perfect backdrop to the 'party,'
and men dancing with men
openly affectionate, so natural as couples.
And two girls in the corner in each other's arms.
Evie moved through in a trance,
it seemed perfectly normal in one way
and yet... she was as yet too uncool!
She felt so limited as if the world
at large, no matter what she read,
or to whom she talked,

late nights over wine or in lecture halls,
in movie houses or bookshops,
the world at large was still at large!

And I in my small corner (where Jesus bid me shine)
 as she'd sung countless times as a little thing
at Sunday school in perfect tune.
Still in her small corner!
Uncool... her life was still too suburban, too small!
It made her vaguely angry.
Still on the cusp of knowing, really knowing.

Strange that Jenny unknowingly
was introducing her to another world,
effortlessly, carelessly even.
Real-life experience out there in the world,
Jenny who in the end was almost defeated
by too much experience of her own
but then fearless
already shaping a new life here,
confident! original!
Both these friends enmeshed in their art
In art, all of their lives, as she was with words.
As if there is no other way to live.
(as if you had any choice).

Funny old Mr Probert and Kings Cross.
Could a fortune teller have foretold
any of it? And would it help to know?
Things like that, people like Rob.
Rob's appearance and reappearance?
What it meant? What it means?

Part 3
Suburbia

*'She had to escape them, all of them
and the place, that's all she knew'*

Doing time in the burbs…

What is the happy comfort of the familiar?
Remembering those younger girl friends
long afternoons with hair dye and makeup decisions
bursts of laughter repeating old poems
but especially chanting old jingles
Sing-a-long of long gone jingles together
A scrap of your gone self grasped at,
comforting but more than that
consoling and funny at the same time.

Like the 5-point Ampol service jingle they all sang lustily
We wash your windscreen clean as a slate
Water level is checked while you wait
Then your oil and water pressure too
And finally we pump up your tyres for you!
And in the times of so few cars too
when a garage attendant in white overalls
filled your car and your tyres.

Sip, sip, sip. Bonnington's Irish Moss with
 Pectoral Oxymel of Carrigeen (opium)
Sounding so professional and medical.
And the sexy female voice promising
that a Pelaco shirt definitely
and without question, the best!
It is indeed a lovely shirt, sir.
When the wireless pumped out advertisements
 a cup of tea, a Bex and a good lie down
Gusts of laughter at the memory.

We're resurrecting a world,
the world of the former everyday
with some derision, with a lot of humour,
derisive of the times, mocking of our innocence
laughter at the shock of its dire familiarity.

You are forever acquainted with those words
Forever and ever amen.
Other scraps, the screeds even the creeds
of some adolescent church going time,
Therefore with angels and archangels
And all the company of heaven
We laud and magnify Thy glorious name
Ever more praising thee.
Imprinted in the brain like the poems
you lisped in babyhood and recited
in school recitation groups, with you forever.
Nymph, nymph, What are your beads?
Green glass Goblin. Why do you stare at them
Give me your beads, I want them
No!
Then I shall lie in the reeds and howl all night
For your green glass beads. I love them so
Give them me! Give them me!
No!

Old times Rob Connor did not know
could not share as old friends did.
The time before that helped make her.
Not to be shared now except with the pond
in this garden of the world,
this garden of Totti's and Toby's,
reminiscences coming fast.

A wedding

Her friend Marelle's wedding.
The wedding that so entrapped the girl
and released Evie at the same time.
Evie remembered in her first year at College,
knowing she didn't want to be like
her friend, getting married so hastily
or the girls in the street, leaving school
at the Intermediate Certificate
with their hope 'chests' and
their girlish breasts brim full of hopes;
their lace-edged pillow cases, and linen tea towels,
their private dreams with babies dandled in them.

Why wasn't she like these people in any way?
Or was she like them?
She was embarrassed by their ordinariness
even Totti and Toby in their finest, that night,
at friend Marelle's wedding, her favourite aunt and uncle
beaming at them all, her mother delicate and beautiful,
her father always happy in a circle of men,
'Nothing like a wedding!' Embarrassed.

And those resentful neighbours too,
mistrustful of the distance
she was already putting between them.
Girls don't really need to go to university...
How would it be to live a life in a suburb,
the street pretty much your world?

Where divorce was a word that was whispered
when nervous breakdowns, women only,
(Forget the returned soldier
who sat on the fence in the sun
and stared at his hands for hours
or sometimes cried, softly cried,
remembering god knows what?)
were part and parcel of street life,
the street gossip
where she tended to remember
a parade of the oh so ordinary, the envious,
and the small-minded;
and not so much moments of generosity
and kindnesses of which there were many.

She should try to remember,
offerings small and large;
the home cooked dinner for the bereaved,
the layette for the young wife
coming home with first baby,
the willing help, heads in car bonnets
or half bodies under cars
to help share knowledge
of fixable greasy car engines,
the modest shared pride in the new carpet
or washing machine, a wonder of a thing;
let alone the marvel of television,
it's arrival, a communal affair.

She'd seen the odd
black and white television arrive
to the street

the wonder and the envy.
(though it was widely known they already had colour
in America and it wouldn't be long in coming.)

Oh the arrival of that so anticipated furniture!
Well it was furniture, a sleek wooden cabinet
with a highly polished surface and brass door handles
revealing the curved screen and the magic of movies
in your own home! Stories and news and documentaries,
affecting the bookcase for all time.

Her father in his haste
to get it home from *Eric Anderson's Electricals*
borrowed a small utility to deliver it himself
to a gaggle of kids so eagerly waiting.
Easy, easy down the black hill and faster
through a couple of flat wide streets,
bent on getting it home and getting it on!
But taking on the last corner into their street
too fast and too eager,
the unwieldy piece of furniture tipping over
shattering the longed-for screen.
Long faces up and down the street.
No miracle tonight!

Yes, the sharing that went on.
The generous sharing of knowledge,
'I'll teach her piano,'
'I'll make his birthday cake.'
'I'll lend you the money.' Over and over.
Small kindnesses. Unrecorded by her.
Why not? What was wrong with her?

The older folk who offered bright scraps of their lives
in front yards to small children
playing on the verges and 'wise saws',
and plain affection in their cakes with white icing
and twisty topped meringues.
Hair-plaiting, titivating and family tales.
Yes, if she tried not too hard, she could conjure up
those affections but there was shame in it, in them.
She had to escape it all the same.

And her friend's wedding finished the place
once and for all. Nervous Melly as she was called
but not so nervous as to get pregnant one summer
to the most handsome boy in the neighbourhood
danced with at the church social
and co-extensive with, in the Maroubra sandhills,
once a raceway for speed happy spectators
and often an escape for young lovers.

And Lee, the old leering fool who'd approached the bride
on her wedding night to kiss her full on the lips
and tell Mella he knew she was no virgin,
then likewise, that same old bugger had leaned forward
so that he could tell Evie too,
'I seen you slutting, m'dear!
In the car late night, I seen you under the streetlight.'
the surge of his alcoholic breath, repellent
as his desirous eyes.
What made this shambles of a man need to be so cruel?

'Disgusting old letch,' as Francie
from up the road had called him.

in no uncertain words. 'A real creep.'
Francie who came to stay in short bursts
with an 'auntie' up their street a few houses away,
the first child she'd ever known
except in storybooks who was an orphan.
No mother and no father! Abandoned!
Or as a neighbour had labelled her
'She's a state ward and looks it with that haircut!'
State ward, a frightening description
meaning no one much wanted Francie.
This was a girl who talked loudly and carelessly,
swearing if she wanted to, even the F word too,
and ran with the boys mostly
her long thin legs easily
outstripping some of the fastest
and the strongest of them,
earning their respect,
yet not quite their friendship.
She was after all still a girl,
but no interest in playing skippings rather
play marbles, the boys' game and played it well.
And this stripling of a girl despite herself
had grown into a slender beauty
that old man Lee soon spotted and delayed
whenever he could, with threats and then money.

She felt sorry for Francie,
sorry for poor Marelle and her forced union,
handsome or not handsome husband.
Now Mella would never get to the teacher's college,
she'd anxiously, secretly planned for
against her parents' advice.

Evie had to escape them, all of them
and the place, that's all she knew!
And yet the memory of softer quieter moments,
some funny, tender memories, eh?
And the innocence of so many of them,
Her own innocence.

But then that over-reaching guilt!
It made her angry again.
The guilt that girls and women were made to feel
for the transgression of making love- not making war mind!
'Love, love, love! that the flower children enshrined in song!
As if society had you pinioned - that kind of girl
with no comparison for - that kind of boy,
A reverse really- that kind of boy/man in admiration.
or the contempt for the divorced woman
in the street 'living in sin!' Who had the temerity
to go about her shopping, go about her life
as if she were normal!
Evie only knew she had to escape it, them, all of it!

Loves past

The pond was doing this unfurling,
memories surfacing like wraiths,
misty then not, from dark bountiful waters.
Henry first lover now? Or Lucas and her affair?
Her heart seemed to squander several loud beats.
Not yet.
Alpha and omega first and last. Last?
Henry first lover, then Tom her only husband.
The only one she'd married!
And no, she wouldn't think of Henry now
and that almost innocence. Or of Tom and marriage.

There was a caterpillar and should she
flick it or leave it for the butterfly thing.
Why would she flick it for the leaf's sake?
And presently they'd call from the verandahh
into that yellow glow of the lit up house
and she'd have to leave the pond
To be in safely, to be re-affirmed, boring
Familiar. And safe.
But not yet, not yet.
Nature rampant and things eating
and being eaten constantly
munching and masticating devouring
each other!
And Lucas illicit lover persisting.
He didn't devour her
No, it was she who devoured him

with her too romantic notions of love
and her urgent need for tender love-making
and then not so tender.

She wanted to think about love
Defined in so many ways by poets and writers
often as a madness. Or a stupor, or a trance?
Was it love that bound her to a marriage?
Her marriage to Tom.
Should she go through that circuitous corridor?

Totti and Toby

She looked up at the house
hoping now they would call her,
willing it,
yet unable to leave.
It must be time for something
a drink, the pre-dinner time talk,
watching uncle's wrinkled hands
and the black onyx ring set in thick gold, he favoured,
winking across the room as he
poured the whiskey, and listening to the comfort
of their voices discussing things,
even the horror of that war.
That bloody unnecessary war.

He'd always begin the same way
and their friend from Taree
their farmer friend,
who'd lost a bloody good son
in Vietnam a foreign place
nothing to do with them or his farm
or his family, and what for?
And Toby actually making a growling sound,
growling like a bear over words like
incendiary and defoliation and Viet Cong,
and Totti letting it roll, shaking her head sadly
in agreement, until a draught of whiskey
a change of tone. A long sad sigh and then a brightening

Jack the yellow canary, and its antics outside its cage.
Great big Toby always respectful of this tiny dot of bird
as it perched on his finger, affectionate and admiring
This dot singing its heart out – and your own, she thought
sometimes not coping with the bird brilliance,
its cascades of sound, the highest yellow note,
as Van Gogh had called yellow summer
in the south of France, hadn't he?
Slender pale yellow bird singing its heart out
Higher rills of it, sweet, sweeter, sweetest, impossibly so…

'and they're racing...'

Then Totti relating her 'herbaceous escapade'
as she called it in the garden today among
weeds and coming abundance, so much to do in Spring.
And knowing in the morning
they both might take her on tour
down the crazy path out back, only just passable,
and point out something twining, blossoming,
a weedy pot plant or two, sudden coloured blooms,
until the creaky table and chairs in a pool of dappled light,
the Saturday Table, as Totti had called it,
where they both sat so much a pair
smoking from their daily ration of cigarettes
or Toby drawing on his pipe,
long happy exhalations and exaltations
something so deeply satisfying to be had
even their movements co-ordinated,
their bright eyes, predictions, hopes
and a special language
as they pored over the racing form,
bible-studious, transistor radio at the ready.

The staunch attention
 as the strains of their favourite caller,
 Ken Howard's nasal authoritative voice
jarred on the air, so riveting, they sat
studied and motionless
 until the end of his incantation.
 Once Totti had apologised to her
'Toby needs the call be so loud!'

She told them she didn't mind
the Saturday blur of sound
 Ready to leave the birdcage,
and they're racing!
That familiar adenoidal voice that rose and rose on the air,
(Not mindful of the canary trill but as loud),
About a length and a half
Moving in just behind....
And now into the strait
A furlong and a half to go...
Then a gap to-
At the head of the others...
Coming home hard...
As horses strained to exceed their own capabilities,
and the race caller just about burst his boiler,
in the excitement as a winner tore home,
a crescendo as the first three names were sung out,
coming down the scale while the later horses came in.
Sighs and the odd swear word
or a gratifying cackle of laughter
as they estimated losses and rewards.

'You should try to paint horses,' Toby had told her
most beautiful of creatures, after canaries that is!
Or write a poem...'

Totti said, 'you should finish that poem
you started.' She chose to look blank.
'The poem about families.' She frowned
There's no poetry left she tried to explain.
'Not a sausage,' she joked. But Totti said,

'I saw it on your desk yesterday, love.'
Now she blushed like a child. 'That's old stuff.
It didn't work Totti. Doesn't work.'

She'd only really talked seriously about poetry
at college to a teacher who favoured her,
time to time to her close school friend,
but most of all, so strange to say, to Rob Connor!
Trying to make sense of her little life
 describe her feelings... her family
scattered or dead or indifferent now,
It was so bloody painful.
and here was Totti who only truly valued bush ballads
and could cheerfully recite Banjo's Snowy River poem.
'There was movement at the station
for the word had passed around
that the colt from old Regret had got away
and joined the wild bush horses
he was worth a thousand pounds
So all the cracks had gathered at the fray...'
Or Kendall's Bellbirds making her think of her mother
By channels of coolness the echoes are calling
And down the dim mountains I hear the creek falling
And softer than slumber and sweeter than singing
The notes of the bellbirds go running and ringing.
Among other verses and bush snippets
 telling Evie to go on with her writing, as if it were important.
'It just isn't working,' she tried to explain.

Part 4
Writing

'so words spill and watchwords gather unimpeded'

When she writes…

Things scrawled easily by wind or stick
or sodden leaf on water here.
Evie watched their easy gait.
And why, why couldn't she write now?
was squandering time?
She'd heard of writers' block
knew those who boasted of it,
to her unimaginable. Words had aways been so easy
Why then this lull? What the fear?
She couldn't stay here forever entranced
at a pond with scarcely moving water?
Her mirror?

Rob Connor had read one of two poems
he'd found in her student notebook,
had asked her to write him a letter.
Tended to write letters then, she mused,
smiling at the idea, a letter
telling him exactly how she felt
in the act of creation, how she went about
her poems. It was almost invasive
so private an experience, self-absorbed
in the poetry trance as she tried to explain
but a grand assignment
in which she reached for honesty
for him of course for him and – well
to impress the man but in doing it
she found it was mostly for herself.

She'd kept that scribbled thing too
and his reply.

Inside one dreary afternoon she'd cleared out her desk
and found it in green tooled leather hold-all,
for the time when pen and ink had been chosen
and she'd found an old fountain pen, a Conway Stuart
and even affected purple ink
pleasing feeling, pen in hand,
light on the upstrokes and heavy on the down.
She'd unfolded it and carefully smoothed it
so she wouldn't tear the age-stained paper
and read it
to try to remember that exact feeling
she'd so easily and loosely captured for him.

Dear Rob,
When I write,
everything present seems to backdrop.
Gazing unseeing into the distance
phrases rather than words
jump to mind mysteriously satisfying.
There's effort in the thinking,
pleasure in it, so words spill
and watchwords gather unimpeded.
Sometimes a super awareness, music,
a bird call can seem a deliberate
even rapturous accompaniment
to thoughts, reaching out after newness,
freshness her own closeted individuality.
A power in the word and unexpected phrase,
as if you are imbued with a strange convincing capacity,

and in a trance of language
where you, and only you can exact,
that precise meaning of those precise moments.

Otherworldly and yet somehow steeped in realness
intensely personal
almost beyond you but with pen in hand, not.

(She smiled as she read it but her heart
contracted as if there were truly something lost.)
And knowing later that this rhapsody,
you were lucky enough to experience
(like the love rhapsody)
didn't necessarily promise you a magnum opus,
though you believed at the time it did!

She'd written so many poems
liked to record her life with them, not for publication.
So why no words now. Words about, but not words
from a 'sacred brook or beck' as someone,
was it Keats? had said. A bit much 'sacred,'
And sacred re-arranged could so easily be 'scared'.
A little fear was in it too, she thought,
this tributary that could become torrent.
What could she find here? Some good?

"And this our life, exempt from public haunt,
finds tongues in trees,
books in the running brooks,
sermons in stones, and good in everything."

Tom and marriage

Tom. She had to re-think Tom.
Or just think Tom, the man she chose to marry!
She remembered she had written a poem for him
on their engagement
wrested from her suffocating love for him.
Terrible word engagement, engaged,
a word that came up on doors of toilet cubicles,
taken, something removing you from freedom.
I do not bring a gift of value,
Only myself, singing down open-gladed colours.
How could she have been so glad and so pathetic?
How could she feel so worthless to write such words?
and yet she remembered the rush of happiness
It was sad...so keen to be in bondage?

Tom didn't comment on the poem, perhaps indifferent?
Swept away, his urgent passionate love-making,
his verve, his fixatedness, his energy for life, love.
She was not so much captured as swept up and away
as if on a Bondi breaker roiling and boiling its way to shore.
Tom of the loving, of the dark anger
and unexpected tenderness,
Tom of the boyishness, of the cruelty,
of the resentment and protectiveness.
Tom. Of the perplexing suddenness.
Of the desire to have and to hold and to own.
Of the lovingness, the passion that could turn on a coin
to a sudden rage!

She held back her dreams from him and he knew it.
He raged against her understandings, her friendships
that seemed to close him out.
Fury at being locked out of part of her,
and then all of her.

Rosie, his child

There was a time way back suddenly sharp.
in her mind, that night
when Rob Connor suddenly had money,
a comfortable amount of money.
His friend Reece had told Evie at one of Clea's parties,
'It happens on rare occasions and you never ask.
He's flush for a few months at least.'
He'd sought her out. 'Evie we're dining tonight!'
A dinner in a small bar, a cleft in the Rocks,
a slice of harbour glinting and serene
under the ugly concrete of elevated train tracks
that had uglified Circular Quay.

Adelaide had come good at last, he told her.
'Sit by the window Evie, in the harbour view
'Any wine you like my darling...'
and a slight shifting of the mask,
showing her the remnants of his long-over marriage.

A small creased photograph, a child in a stroller.
'It's all I have,' he joked. Maybe not joking,
a sweet-faced child, his little girl
dark-eyed like he was,
and pretty as small children are
with their chubby grasping hands,
with their frank unerring gaze, pretty
like the unknown mother, surely.
'She stole her away,' he said, vehemently.

'She stole Rosie away.'
With his first glass of wine, sadly serious now.
'Working away I was for both of them, all of us!
in the city and getting home late most nights,
one night, oh night of nights, to an empty house!
Not just my wife and my child gone, my darling,
everything gone, every stick of furniture
every painting, every knife, fork and wine glass
lock stock and barrel gone.
My clothes in a heap on the floor
you can't imagine!'
He was deep breathing at the memory.
'But the worst of it, Evie, the worst,
Rosie, my baby girl, Rosie gone.
I lay on the floor, she couldn't take the carpet,
it was fixed to the wooden floor
and hell, Evie,' he took her hand and crushed it
in his, 'hell I cried like a baby.'

Her heart ached for him.
She liked the strength of his grasp
and returned it, asking something,
'So you still see your little girl?
'Surely? You still see Rosie? Your rights?'
His face set hard. 'Rights? None, my dear.
What's worse she left Sydney.
She went back to Adelaide,
to her interfering family.' He sighed.
photo carefully placed inside his wallet.
'She would be five now - yes five at least...'
He wasn't sure.

That night in her own bed she reflected
that Rob Connor had a photo of his daughter,
a two year old in a pram, realising
that he hadn't tried too hard then
to find his only daughter,
to know the sweet-faced Rosie,
now perhaps four years old,
with a sweet-faced mother,
or maybe even five years old
somewhere lost in Adelaide.

Darlinghurst Rob

All these Rob memories she couldn't push aside
as if reaching back for some understanding. As if
she might find some 'logic' to love, to love affairs.

That other come-by-chance meeting
Rob Connor himself, a year or so later
after Clea, after Cressy.
Ah no, not Cressy with him, his bride, his prize.
On the gritty pavement neon-lit she saw him
in Darlinghurst Road, seeking the restaurant with
the giant schnitzels her friend Reece so loved.
Lena's near Bar Coluzzi.
It always seemed to her Rob came
out of a dream
There he was, Rob Connor, tall, pale and handsome,
a serious-faced dumpy woman on his arm,
then a smiling Rob Connor, rushing forward,
arms outstretched to both of them.
'Ah Reece! Ah Evie!'

 And Rob insisting gaily, 'Haven't seen you and Reece in ages.'
Picking up their lives as if a few of weeks had gone by.
'Come to Delia's flat just down the way,
That's okay Delia isn't it?
They're old best friends of mine- both?'
She saw the pursed lips and the flash of anger
and then the woman's nod of acquiescence.
As they filed upward ill lit stairs,
Cressida's name on her lips.

'Terrible business,' he whispered later, 'Cressy's folks
got a private eye. Spying. Imagine on little old me.
Dug up stuff and invented half of it
Sheer hell I can tell you!'
He didn't say *all of it*, she noted.
'Fed her with lies, bloody terrified her.
Daddy ended it for us with not so choice words.
and scared the shit out of me.'

'I've got to admit. Effective threats.
Found every book I'd given.
every gift in a neat pile on my stairs.
They'd taken her overseas little Cressy.
Like a Victorian novel for God's sake
off shore to get over evil me.
Poor little pet of a thing, I didn't even get to explain...'

And Delia?
There was no time. Ahead of them
Delia was holding open the door to her life.
'She can sing, by God but she can sing!
Wait till you hear Delia sing...'
Wanting to turn away
to leave Delia and her singing
and the smiling, urging Rob Connor.

The flat was ugly and purplish,
the settee old fashioned and hard.
Cramped, shabby, even the prints on the wall
were brownish and limpid. Characterless.
Sound effects from the bathroom too.

Delia urinating, heavy like a horse,
hard for all to bear. They raised their voices.
Who had designed such a place?
How was the elegant Rob Connor holed up here?
With crinkly cream wall paper and heavy picture rails?

She wanted to leave but Rob was insistent.
Reece went away for wine and Delia
found biscuits and hard cheese served
on a thick plate missing a sprig of anything
and they settled into her singing,
and his obsequiousness.

She wanted to cry for what he'd become.
Cry despite the voice, like cut glass.
Cut glass.
One of her aunt's cut glass came suddenly to mind.
Glasses always resplendent in the
bow-fronted piece of furniture referred to
respectfully as the china cabinet, with no china at all
but with glasses, she remembered, collections of them.
'Crystal,' the preening aunt had told them
when she and her mother unwillingly visited,
taking some, one by one, to hand around,
'Waterford, my dears. And this one, best quality Stuart.
Heavy you see. Four no five lots of them.'
Looking slyly at Evie then her mother
as they were handed back carefully,
'And some of them for you, Evie. Eventually.'
Placed extra carefully with an unpleasant flourish
beside their flock, their legion? She couldn't think of the word.
Anyway, when does 'eventually' come, she wondered,

and would she care for a legion of glasses
when it did, Waterford or Stuart? Crystal or not?

Clear, full throated, cutting and beautiful
Delia's voice like cut glass and Rob,
Rob of the frayed cuffs and scuffed shoes
and smiling face descending into fatness,
Rob and Delia. No!

Part 5
The Blue Mountains

"And I yield to it absolutely," but it was more than love.'

Suddenly Henry

Then back, back again over the water,
a slight breeze rippling the pond,
the cool of the afternoon descending
and Henry, suddenly darling Henry,
tender and loving student Henry.
Now she welcomed thoughts of Henry.

Why hadn't she stayed with him?
Dreamy grey-green eyes, thick curly hair ,
high forehead, witty rejoinders,
a kind of intellectual snobbery about him,
unreasonable jealousy of her poetry writing,
bright articulate gentle Henry.
That was first love surely. A first
serious relationship.

She remembered parking on a cliff at Bondi Beach
and all the thrilling foreplay of first love
as thrilling as it could be inside a small car
with bucket seats and the fear of prowlers,
A flock of birds nearby taking off
in the yellow-white sheen of street light,
and a line of poetry coming
sweet as his kisses at that moment.
And our dreams shall go up together
Like a flock of birds
Scribing furiously at home.
Remembering that moment forever

and the shock of her disengagement
and words forming at all
when she felt such a rush of love for him.
His Europeanness, his love for her.

She, coveting of a figurine, a small ivory elephant
on the shelf in his booklined bedroom,
let alone the volume of Rainer Maria Rilke poetry.
He, laughing and refusing, then later gifts made
to her of both those treasures.
She still had the Rilke.
*'and you yourself, above my heart, beloved
entered upon a kind of wildest childhood'*
He read from it aloud, his love apparent.
*"I want to be with those who know secret things
or else alone."*

She wasn't altogether ready for Henry.
That must have been it.
He was so loving, engaging,
his love-making so gentle.
She would have to hurt him, deeply hurt him.

His letter of several pages part of it penned from the tower
in Sydney University where he climbed in a frenzy
maybe even to jump! he told her, was unbearable.
His hurt, his feeling of betrayal when she told him
she'd met Tom and was leaving him.
How could she tell him
she was already grieving for him, for Henry
so much part of her life,
their growing up together.

How could she say she wanted both!
He sent her the Yevtushenko poem
they had both loved so much.
They'd heard the poet in the Sydney Town Hall,
the miracle of a Russian poet
coming all the way to Australia
to read his poems in Russian, immediatly translated.
The magic. One of them was called *Colours*
and later Henry read it aloud to her.

When your face
appeared over my crumpled life
at first I understood
only the poverty of what I had.
Then its particular light
on woods, on rivers, on the sea
became my beginning in the coloured world
In which I had not yet had my beginning.
I am so frightened, I am so frightened,
of the unexpected sunrise finishing,
of revelations
and tears and the excitement finishing.

'the pilgrim soul in you'

Student parties with Henry and picnics
and the guitar no one could play,
the flute he tried so ineptly to play.
His obvious jealousy of her at the piano,
flinging out her ill-played Bach or Chopin
for his pleasure first of all
and then vague displeasure...

No one had thought to have him taught an instrument
of any kind at all! He railed about his mother,
His refugee doctor mother, fierce and outspoken,
so very bright and determined to succeed
in this strange hot peaceful place, in Sydney.
She had taken the necessary medical exams in Latin
not having much English when she first arrived,
in Australia. Polish wartime refugee,
so she could practice in Australia
earn a living and give thanks for their survival,
His mother,
(who'd called him Henry because Henry
was safely non-European). His mother
who'd not been overly welcoming to her.
Tolerated her, Evie thought,
who'd once as the doctor she was, examined her breasts
on some trumped up excuse, of her
seeming to be retaining fluid, fingers and ankles,
easy to fix as if she were a damaged thing,
to be fixed, perfected,

and told her victoriously, '- an invaginated nipple!
You won't suckle children easily, my dear!'
finalising her disapproval.
Her humiliation knew no bounds...
but she had shrugged it off, and wondered
at his mother's sore need to possess.

Not a surprise she reasoned later,
given where she'd come from
what she'd escaped. 'Gas ovens,' Henry had explained
'I shouldn't be here.' And smiled his boyish confiding smile.
And then of how his mother fought to keep her son.
Suffering and bravery bred a survival hardness,
her steely aspiration. Admirable woman,
but a mother to be avoided nonetheless.

The fluid tablets she'd been given by his mother
did it, she was certain.
In a hot crowded flat where they were dancing
all of them Henry's friends
Bodies pressed close, loud music and swooning faces
or so they seemed the moment before the blackness.
The collapse and crowd parting
and Henry, tender Henry to the rescue
at first to the lounge and then outside
to recover, to deep breathe
in the cool air where she rested against Henry
breathing deep and then rummaged a moment
in her bag feeling for the bottle of tablets.
At first opportunity, she threw them into the gutter.

She still had the book Henry inscribed with W.B. Yeats' poem

How many loved your moments of glad grace,
And loved your beauty with love false or true,
But one man loved the pilgrim soul in you,
And loved the sorrows of your changing face;

Blue, Blue Mountains and Henry

'Pilgrim soul.' She loved that description.
The first time in the Blue Mountains with Henry,
seemed to engulf her in its blue haze and pungent scent
of eucalypt forests, cajoling again.
When they'd read Sir Gawain and the Green Knight
and why not an Australian poem she wondered idly?
But that would come later
when she was penning so many poems herself.

Sitting on a high rock that was somehow flung
halfway down a valley, jutting up out of green
tracts of trees, stiff ferns and repeating outcrops,
impossible not to climb this one,
and spread out in the pale sun. And Gawain.
The books with biscuits and a flask, he'd carried.
Was it wine, did they even drink then, or was it coffee?
Anyway a picnic on a rock and then love-making,
the rock up and away and swirling them together
airborne must have been, for hours on end.
That was when he'd tried to say forever
And she'd turned away, turned another page.

They'd walked every afternoon the same way,
down a curling bush track near the house to the lookout,
where they'd always kiss and then hold the cold iron rail
that kept them from another precipitous edge,
look in wonder yet again.
One blustery afternoon they had to lurch their way

to the lookout, faces smitten with cold,
coats wrapped tightly, scarves flying
As they stood bodies feeling frail in the wind
Henry yelled something that was swept away.
'Whaat?'she called and he stood closer.
'Yield to it, Evie! Yield, my darling!"
The night before they'd been reading Rilke again
One of the love poems that ended
His way weepingly through you he's wending
Yield to him. Do not say nay,
That had made their love-making even more passionate.

'I love that word yield,' she yelled back, 'I love this place!
And I yield to it absolutely.'
Her heart was full these moments but it was more than love
for Henry rocking in autumn wind close against her.
That afternoon a sudden power
seemed to course through her body
because of the ruling wind, yes, its gusting and keening,
and the splendid shining rutted rockfaces
and the mighty spreading out valley below
and the small mountains far far away,
gradations of blue on blue.
Two small figures on a cliff top.
Two inconsequential figures.
Hearts full with the sweep of the valley
from valley floor to sky
gulping the valley
the green sap of a million trees
running wild with sap that she felt course through them,
Her windswept body. And his.
'Yield to it, Evie.' And she did. They both did.

The absence of Henry, the cut,
the brutality of the idea of parting
the grieving for him, for them
even as she was drawn inexorably to another,
the tumult of heart
aware, if only she were not,
of his longing for her of his pain and loss.
And long moments of the very same pain
for her, the one precipitating the parting.
How could she do it?
How could she do this to him?
How?
And yet she did, she had.
He had foretold it, hadn't he
The sorrow of her changing face.

Wine bar

Rob Connor, in one of the sudden flash wine-bars
that sprang up welcomed all through Sydney
as if Sydney was having a taste of Europe or New York
A wine bar on north shore. With her husband now.
With Tom late afternoon.

Why were they even there since
Tom hardly had a drink. A wine bar. Very posh.
Not long married.
Then Rob Connor a figure appearing
Out of years gone by,
Out of the gloom against a backdrop of shaded lights
and glinting bottles, glasses clustering,
and the slightly dank smell of underground,
Wine cellar and bonhomie.
And Rob Connor
out of a past Tom did not, would not ever know.
Perched on a stool, handsome in a flabby way
tossing back his dark hair and another drink
and greeting her, them, eagerly.
He talked easily and loudly and Tom nodded
a stiff acceptance of this unknown man
to her relief. Even accepted a drink.
Haphazard talk but questions on her mind, so many.

'Have I ever showed you this, Tom?'
As if he knew Tom from some other time.
'This is my baby girl, this is Rosie.'

And the creased photograph appeared
for Tom's uninterested glance.
Rob Connor touched her arm,
his expression querulous when they took their leave.
Who was the last partner, the dowdy singer from Darlinghurst
whose name had escaped her? He seemed sadly alone.
This time she wanted to reach out to help him
and that's all. No stars and giddy pavements.
No wild plans and talks and songs. Brides to be.

But Tom would mind any delay
and they had so much to discuss,
her pregnancy for one thing.
'Who in the hell was that creep?' Tom asked her.
As they drove through Lavender Bay.
Heading back towards familiarity of the east.
'Gay boy for sure.'

Max of Matra

Gay boy.
It had been Max who'd reached out to her
through all the terrible tirade of bad news
Her mother's suicide and its aftermath for
all of them. Max the tall, lean, almost-handsome hairdresser.
Max whose history helped him stand firm with empathy.

He'd related some of his ugly high school days
as he arranged and re-arranged her hair,
she delaying to spend more time with him
or to hear him like The Ancient Mariner,
having to tell his story over and over again.
Max. His life. His schooldays out near the
drive-in theatre at Matraville, near the Botany cemetery,
the most unfashionable part of the eastern suburbs
of Sydney. Surely! His story.
Before he'd properly known, he said, that he was gay
though they, the boys in his school knew all too well.

The school morning he found to his amazement
his name painted on the outside toilet walls in livid pink,
beside a pink cartoon by a not unskilled hand.
Poofta wrongly spelled. His name correctly managed.
The laughter, his anger and his shame. In the classroom
the chairs thrown at him, once a teacher left,
bus rides with shoving and kicking and pushing
until he decided to walk, the long sandy route home
a better option past the Chinese market gardens

where someone looked up from his work
and always waved to him.
where he waved back
thinking he wanted to be a market gardener
that was for sure. All day out in the open
mostly alone except for veggies. Heaven!
And why wasn't he Chinese, with a father
who was a market gardener?

Then home...
His father's anger, his pep talks,
his advice 'to stand up to it like a man!'
His father's angry unwilling visit to the school
that seemed to make things worse.
The unaccountable days when
almost unspoken serious bullying was agreed upon,
when everyone in his form or that's how it seemed
would strike out at him in some way, on principle.
And the small weak kids who took no part
or those who had no taste for blood
would drop their eyes when he moved past
dabbing a cut lip or tucking in a torn shirt,
as if he was not visible.
Invisible he thought, but not for the haters.

The slow grind of years hiding
(but not always) from the worst of them.
Finding a friend or two.
A teacher or two making the difference,

making room for him to be a splinter of someone,
telling him there's more education to be had outside,
and half-believing, hoping, biding his time,
until his escape from his schooling at last.
And the night he'd discovered he liked boys
in such a pleasurable not-to-be mistaken way.
Arriving at the party, his girlfriend away somewhere,
the music, the flashing anticipation and pressing crowd,
a shortish attractive man, muscular and smiling,
suddenly beside him, taking his hand
and out on the stair-well with the dark sweep of Bondi Beach
not far distant, the thrum of waves nearby,
kissing his lips full on
and the shock of desire he'd never known like this,
thrilled from head to foot so that he began shaking,
wanting to grab at the stranger, be taken away by him
to be fucked silly by him, compliant desirous,
awash with joy and filled with questions
for the insistent stranger, though neither spoke,
who soon disappeared into the crowd again
leaving an ecstatic troubling knowledge
as if with that explosive kiss,
his manhood, all that he was and could be,
found, corroborated at last,
the stranger was simply saying,
'There, now you understand, Don't you?'
And he did. His desire, his virility, his confusion.
Home on winged feet. Longing to tell.
Perhaps his sister but was she too young
to quite understand. Telling no one.

Max of Taylor Square

Something known but never surfaced, never uttered,
was uttered at last, the unutterable, but not at home.
Silent for the family's sake. His father's most of all.
Another year. Surreptitious meetings.
A growing manhood, the secret joy and fear.
Another year. His father unhappily accepting 'hairdressing'
'Couldn't you be a barber. I'd help set you up!'
His mother furtively understanding. His sister encouraging
him in every way she could, mostly silently.
Jokes at breakfast and no invitations to the RSL
until his father grudgingly accepted
'A queer, very queer son.' That humourless laugh.

Years piling up for Max
whose father still hoping, would definitely set him up
in his own business if he 'got better,'
went to a psychologist who could set him straight
He'd heard of one right here in the eastern suburbs,
successful too. More than one lad come good!

Max who'd seemed to understand Evie's pain instinctively,
The unbearable weight of someone's suicide,
let alone it being your mother's.
The way she found she could talk more freely to him
than most of her friends, all sympathetic
but not quite understanding in the way
Max seemed to intuit. There was just some relief
in being able to say her name, 'my mother'

and relate some happier incident, or any incident,
none of the sad details needed.
No explanation just being able to say the words
'My mother Colleen, her name is Colleen.
My mother, my mother, my mother.'
And Max's hand on her shoulder,
his eyes meeting hers in the mirror as she stared
first into his kind eyes and then beyond.

Max, who'd left so suddenly and so forever.
Why think of him? His appetite for life,
his kindness. Max of the long artistic fingers,
and the way she could talk so freely to him.
Think impossibility!

Max philosophising on love, life and hair colour,
who should have been here for gay marriage
approval and transgender realisations
But who'd quietly OD'd in his flat in Bondi,
the flat his father had grudgingly
bought him in the end. His death,
overdosing, an error of judgement, they said,
like the artist Brett Whitley for sure.
Except that he, Brett being an artist, was famous for it,
taking his own life in the tawdry south coast motel,
an accident for sure.

Max had wanted to take her to gay bars.
'Since you're a writer, for the experience.
Come to Taylor Square see a show
Come to Caps darling.
Dance floor and bar second floor the show!
Maybe the smallest stage best drag show in town.'

She didn't go with him to Caps or Patches
Or Flo's Palace up there.

He'd always be second guessing things about her
bringing her an article about some aging poet or artist
usually but not always gay,
some rich palace gossip or closer to home,
salacious stuff about 'names'
from suburbs round about,
names he couldn't actually name
though sometimes did in a whisper.
And the way he'd ask with that soft voice
when she sank into the chair and
they exchanged their mirror smiles
And how are you, E, today? and she knew
he was quietly acknowledging her ongoing pain
her very mental struggles.

She wished she'd gone with him
to his real side of his life,
to one of those places so important
in his life, something he could share,
which still had to be furtive
and often undercover
but it had never happened
and now could not happen
not even a talk over coffee and a
new colour that would suit you
absolutely perfect for you, E!
Max gone out of this world.
But not the memory of his kindness
when she most sorely needed it.

Henry and friend

Yesterday before the pond time
she had stared at and hated
her visage in the mirror.
Men who had loved her
had called her beautiful.
Like Henry. Like Tom. Like Lucas. Like Rob.
Especially Lucas who'd called her once
standing naked by the window
in an unctuous hotel room
they should not have been in,
called her once, his beautiful Modigliani figure.
And yet right now she remembered
just as clearly the other come-by- chance one
Henry's sometime clever friend Dan,
who'd on first meeting called her 'fuckface.'

And why did his clanging appellation stick in mind?
Danny, scruffy and good-looking
hair curling on his collar
Jutting agro chin, blue-eyes, good looks
he'd visited with friends
Henry's student house in Newtown.
Wine in flagons or cardboard boxes,
or pleasing raffia wrapped bottles
good for candles at late night seances
or poetry readings or talk.

When he'd taken her arm, Evie could still remember
the clutching of Danny's cruel fingers
pressed into her flesh leaving bruises.
How she hated each imprint of him next day
and days that followed.
'No tits either!' he'd announced, 'to speak of,'
trying to swing her round as if she were a specimen, his.
Drilling fingers, hard blue eyes,
an alcohol sneer and an ugly desire.
Let me go! Violence palpable.
Henry came to her rescue. But Danny's words...
'Sure you can have her mate. 'As if he'd made his claim.
'You can have fuckface!'

Henry explained Danny was sick and angry
and always like that when
he was drinking, on weed whatever.
In Henry's bed she couldn't erase the words,
the man, her pitiful inability to reply, defend.
Always like that, Henry murmured as she folded
into the warmth of him, his tender whisperings
but looking in the mirror next day,
she searched her face and wondered
at his fuckface word and at her weakness,
and at a depression that was surely settling.
Mirrors not good, something whispered
Forcing her to look away, walk on by.

Pine forest and mountains

Journeys with Henry, darling Henry,
(could it be she missed him to this day)
but had thrown that love away, in the end.
Or was it the beginning of the harsh learning curve
of what love can do, what it can become.
A thick pine forest outside Canberra
early days of their love affair. Yes,
Henry had been the one accompanied her into adult life.
exchanging books and kisses and readings
and poetry and understandings, patiently,
and with his constant good humour.
Pine trees exuding such a scent,
intoxicating them and the laughter of
freshly realised freedom. Away!

The small car parked out of sight
right under pine branches
as they would camp there in the small canvas tent.
The densely cross-hatched forest floor
mad with quills and spines and needles and
giving such fragrance to the camping site,
so appealingly strong, true to promise,
fortuitously empty of anyone else.
But the fire that wouldn't light and
the darkness suddenly descending
seemed too thick around them,
and the breeze lifting a little.

The sudden prospect of distance
and wildness, even snakes. And forest cold.
Eating biscuits and apples, un-replete in the darkness,
thick darkness even a torch light could not properly pierce.
An untold cold rising up from the fragrant earth
that unsuitable blankets or shivering bodies
close against each other could not exclude.

Laughter but for her an uneasy laughter.
The rising wind in the pine trees seemed
a serious wind that gave the impression
of moving things, creatures,
on the forest floor nearer and nearer...
cold things fingering, ughh!
Giving up on the romance of the forest altogether
to find a roadside motel, *The Rendezvous.*
Of course *The Rendezvous!* Not so far down the road,
and a small and serviceable room was had,
private with its looping nylon lace curtains,
that boasted two trim beds with orange covers,
two badly executed artworks of shacks and gum trees,
and a large print of a Chinese woman of unhappy aspect,
with red red lips, her face with a strangely greenish hue,
hung dispiritingly high on the wall over the bed;
a laminex table, two matching green steel chairs
on a spotty tray teabags and meagre biscuits
only two in a packet, they hungrily devoured.
A lavatory with toilet paper folded to a point
and a paper band over the toilet seat,
assuring them it had been cleaned.

But the prospect of smooth sheets and warm blankets.
More laughter and long love-making,
long sighs, murmurings,
and finally sleep. Our first camping trip.
In the morning exploring the fresh country road,
the feeling that time ahead for them was endless.

Why Henry now?
Those mountain memories with him, too.
Good, good ones, all of them.
The old wooden verandahed mountain house,
his mother had found for them,
eager to stage manage her only son's life.
A gracious deteriorating house
with view down a valley,
rock tiered untidy gardens and some enormous trees.
A holiday house with open fires and open verandahs.
The soft slow massages by candlelight, the pungent oil
and caressing hands and the unbridled joy of love.
Even the uncertainty was delicious in a way,
the gentle tender urging, grasping at the sublime
Moments when you would die for each other
unsaid but contemplated. Can this be true?
Somewhere in the sweeping sensations of these moments
It seemed to be true.

Part 6
The Kiss

*'Liaisons in a lifetime. Shaping a lifetime
Measuring a lifetime.'*

Henry on return

Years after when he saw her again,
a wide sea separating them,
Henry, coming from his English university work,
away from his own newish wife,
for a Sydney conference,
Henry warning her that
he wanted to see her pregnant!
With Tom's child? She knew she still missed him.
Yes, to see her pregnant, and ask her something.
Something that in the end somehow made her cruel
without intending, in her reply.

They'd always spoken honestly to each other...
as the very young find it easier to do,
she ruminated, access to honesty ready...
so she'd tell him honestly,
something extravagant about Tom and his love for her
(not the love-me, love-me, dreadful beat of it)
as she cradled her pregnant stomach,
sitting on a park swing they'd found
near the Balmain restaurant she'd chosen,
where he'd told her about his research,
his new wife, his new life in alien England.
and she noted at the end of lunch,
not asked much about her own life.

The swing was in a park that looked out to the harbour
with its kids' playground and nearby small terraces.

and some fairly ugly industrial stuff,
being softened by the devious fading sunlight.
When she sat awkward in her pregnancy
and rocked back and forth on the swing,
he suddenly asked her the question.
'So I need to ask you this? Why him?'
Staring into that water thoughtfully,
and then into his eyes as the swing brought her
close, closer, poised for a moment,
and then swung her back away from him,
she said quite cruelly, surprising herself,
that she knew, somehow deeply knew
that Tom was a man she thought might die for her!
And meant it! Henry laughed sourly.
'Hard to prove I guess...without someone's tears.'

How could she explain the safety she felt,
the extreme physical protection...
that seemed to mean something, so much
when she'd first known Tom?
Physiologically meant something, must have.
The first time she actually recognised it
was discussing the air balloon accident
somewhere near Canberra that had made the news
for several reasons but mostly because of
of what the surviving wife had said
of her surviving husband, in some wonderment,
'He pushed me back to get up and out!
To save himself! He pushed me back!'
We both made it but everything's changed.'
And the husband mumbling something
about some misunderstanding

120

reaching for her hand that would not be taken,
and that he hadn't done that at all!
But he had. And who could lay blame
for his survival instinct, The lust for life?
What might anyone have done?
What might she have done?

Yet somehow she'd known
Tom would lift her up first,
before any thoughts of himself.
He would run forward rather than away
from imminent dangers if she were beside him.
She knew she had none of that physical courage about anything
Strongman stuff? Super hero stuff?
smiling wryly at the thought.
But it was something deeper, safer, she needed?

Evie knew she was fine with words but weak in action!
Some wonderment at those who did have courage;
some shame in herself for the lack of it.
Ah darling Henry, of the so sad face
I simply did not put you to such
a test in my mind, she thought suddenly.
and why ever not?

On first meeting Rob Connor

Are places revisited almost as critical
as people revisited, she wondered?
When you meet with student friends
there's an ease as of no other time, a carelessness,
an awkwardness too, though something's recognised,
a tacit understanding, a looking out.
The beat before ventures and voyages,
before life opens up and outward,
the teeming edge of things
with all its ardour, all its hope,
hard to quash the hopefulness.
Those places?

What about on first meeting Rob?
Back way back then.
Rob Connor, a striking fellow at a crowded table,
where a friend beckoned her, to join them.
Four or five of them in animated talk.
When she first caught sight of him,
he shifted up for her
to perch beside him as he held forth,
impeccable in his dark suit,
handsome brown eyes, and a shock of dark hair,
including her at the table talk at once,
nervous in her student clothes with her lack of dash,
of beauty, feeling awkwardly young.

Yet, it seemed he sought her out
time and again through their laughing conversations
despite her clothes and too pink scarf, he sought her out.
He entertained the table and she took in his not so secret glances.
She hoped he didn't hear her heartbeat. That no one could.

His non-invitation was impossible to resist.
'If you come back here to the Galleria, say 5 pm tomorrow...
No, on second thoughts little Evie,
don't come back my new little friend.'
He smiled at her
'I'm not exactly trouble, but I'm always heading for it
one way and another.'
He sighed and tapped a cigarette on a smooth skinned packet.
'Dark secrets and too many of them.'
The frown made him even more handsome to her.
'No don't come back to Rowe St,' he whispered.
'I wouldn't advise it.'

His non-invitation to tomorrow, there was no withstanding.
'Believe me sweet child, I'm trouble.'
She wanted to reach out and touch his suited arm
but she smiled and dropped her gaze. Maybe she was blushing.
She arrived a little before five so she could calm herself.
That was the afternoon he first sang to her about Springtime
after she'd got him some coffee and the continental cakes
the Galleria was famous for- she realised
he was hungry and she sat and watched him eat.
Desultory conversation but important things,
his love for poetry for one thing, jazz, record covers,
his need for special cigarettes, female company and music.

'Do I love poetry? Of course I do, as I live and breathe!'
She found herself confessing things to him,
her writing and especially her poetry writing.
'Your poetry to protect you, eh?' he'd asked
and touched her hair so lightly, as if she were
a child thing, an innocent. And she was not!
She'd have to tell him she was not.
But his touch might as well have been a lightning strike
Spring is here! Why doesn't my heart go dancing?
Spring is here! Why isn't the waltz entrancing?
No desire, no ambition leads me
Maybe it's because nobody needs me...

Oh God how sad the words for this big handsome man
to sing to her as they walked up Rowe Street,
beautiful little Rowe Street with its fashionable shops
Sydney's oh so tiny touch of Bohemian life.
Where tea rooms were becoming coffee shops,
with its record shops, with its jewellery shops
one that had buttons beyond compare, a hat shop
and the famous Notanda Gallery prints and painting,
frequented by real live artists, everyone knew it!

As everyone knew a flight down was a bookshop
where you could purchase banned books.
A copy of *Lady Chatterley's Lover* unavailable anywhere else.
except in locked cabinets in English departments in universities,
apparently for the incorruptible academics, they'd laughed at the idea.
His arm around her. Surely the world was at the feet of such a man,
everyone could see her, the girl on the arm of an Adonis.
She would make him happy, she was sure she would.

'You're the poet and I'm the peasant.'
He joked when she shyly read her poems
In the *Poet and Peasant*, a Kings Cross coffee shop
where they met time to time.
'Downstairs to pleasure,' he'd say
Down to this subterranean place
Down into a warmly lit interior.
Coffee and cakes, enjoyed
like a child she thought as
they snatched time together,
the underground-ness of it all
making it seem even more exciting.
Or at the more glamorous *Four Seasons*
Above ground, smack in the middle of the CBD
'Seasons of our lives, darling...'
where in his dark suit he looked,
leaning back against a backdrop of
floor to ceiling frieze of forest trees,
so shockingly beautiful to her.
Rob was only ever revelatory in patches,
his Adelaide family, so gauche
irritating, disappointments there,
and then his quick track to now
and his happiness in being here with her.
She could hardly believe he was here with her
A balancing act...a balancing act for both,
A lifetime ago.

Her own child

Then always Tom overshadowing,
thoughts scattered across a still pond
like the spreading, slowly soaking leaves
that still managed to float,
she had to face him, face it.
Her bewildering submission?

Why did her husband Tom say he didn't want to touch
her pregnant stomach when other
friends said they were caressed by partners?
Yes, partners often kissed the taught skin,
the raised belly button
in wonderment at their growing child?
Spoke to the babe too.
He said it seemed not exactly repulsive
but unattractive, though with the first
stumpy kick she took his hand
to feel the shock of it and despite himself
he was filled with that age old wonder of new life!

Extremes became part of her life, a his'n'hers,
Her love was extreme, a weight for both probably.
His anger was extreme. His lovingness extreme.
She knew fairly soon, especially after gentle Henry
with this man, the often irate Tom, her husband
it was, and always would be, difficult.
Later she reasoned she unwittingly
brought out the worst in him - must have.

Seemed to him she mocked
some deep sense of his worth?
And anger was his weapon.
Rages and unkindness, cruel words. A cruel world
It could seem to her. Then the lickstraps of pleasure,
helpless laughter, helpless love,
the high note of a happiness being with him.
'Walking on air,' understood, high on music and caresses
this too rich brew, animal pleasure and delight
yearning for him and far more, fearing parts of him,
his dark passion, his possessiveness, too.

Love is kind; love does not envy;
love does not parade itself, is not puffed up;
does not behave rudely, does not seek its own,
is not provoked, thinks no evil; does not rejoice in iniquity,
but rejoices in the truth; bears all things, believes all things,
hopes all things, endures all things.

Why had that seemed such a proclamation of truth?
Was it the truth? She loved hearing those words,
so often read out at weddings.
But she had learnt that love is violent too,
plumbs the depths, is measureless, fathomless.
Love can gather you up to madness. Love can be murderous
Love is suffocating, tempting, unreliable.
Love brandishes happiness close at hand, but not.
Love is trickery and anguish and rebuffs
and most of all love turns out to be a series of betrayals.
And yet, alongside all of this, despite all this
love is a list of lilting delights.

The night in their first year of marriage
she felt real fear, when she sensed
some of the unfathomable anger in him
directed so strongly at her.
Tom had left their friend's party,
come home early and annoyed when she'd stayed on,
against his wishes. A flash of anger and he'd left.
Coming home, her key in the door and a mild dread.
Then the assault of the mirror,
their grand cedar mirror
they had been so proud of having found
in an old house, this antique beauty
heavy edged in ruby-red cedar
high and handsome old wood,
over the marble entry table
with his grandmother's Chinese jardinière,
and a precious wooden box, her father's.

The intake of breath, the violence of it,
of him, the sleeping man in their bed ,
to find the word, *lesbian* scrawled on this
and then on every mirror in the house.
Evie the lesbian and other.
As if it were the worst thing he could say...

She'd fallen into bed in the spare bedroom
it too, expectant with its cheerful jungle painting
and its waiting cot for their baby,
wondering what spite drove this mad show of...?
tried to imagine his rage
running from mirror to mirror
like an angry child- no not like a child at all-

and that was surely the horror of it.
Not like a child, but a grown man,
hating her, hurting her as only he could.
Distancing her from him with spite

But the words were miraculously gone
when she woke next morning.
Breakfast to be had, to work early
and were never alluded to. Ever.

Who are you Tom? Who am I?

Now she couldn't stop a rush of memories
and the terrifying night of her late pregnancy,
of the *Braxton Hicks* pains waking her.
Eight months in and she'd read about false labours
named for doctor who explained it was the uterus in practice.
But these sudden frightening contractions
that seemed to be increasing with intensity.
She'd wakened Tom sleeping in the next room
because of her restless pregnant nights.
'What?' furious at being ripped from deep sleep.
'Not time! Don't be ridiculous!'
She'd stood beside the bed arms across her stomach
facing his angry gaze, incensed into silence,
aware she was alone, quite alone in this world.
Doing birth alone!
'Well?' he'd asked angrily. 'What do you want me to do?
'Nothing.' Turning away though the pains were increasing

Back in her room
and she put on a coat
and took up the car keys planning
dramatically, she knew, but
so needy in the dark night
to go across the city to a friend's,
to the hospital, to anyone with sympathy
and away from someone without it!

The car lurched out into the road
and she, crying loudly and despairingly
not with the pains, they were steady strong
which meant she needed help surely,
but crying with the reality of their relationship.

She'd not been able to share much about her pregnancy
as she knew others did with their partners.
He said he didn't want to hear all that stuff.
He was angry she'd let herself fall pregnant
in the first place when they'd planned
to save for another year at least.

Evie instinctively knew she needed him.
She loved him so much, it would be all right.
She knew she needed to humour him too,
through the pregnancy and then surely
it would be all right.
But tonight it wasn't all right!
So where his protective arm now?

On the Gladesville Bridge she saw the petrol gauge
and knew she couldn't make it to the other side
of the city to friends.
And realised at almost the same time with
the diminishing pain of the contractions
the mounting pain of Tom's indifference.
She went back home through the dark hours.
He didn't hear the key in the lock
and just now she couldn't speak to him.
Why didn't she scream, rage, demand?
Why hadn't she? Where was safety now?
She was a weakling, a drama queen?

She lay on her back on the bed, wide-eyed
the great tight mound of baby still now,
as she was. A loneliness welled up in the room
swirled around wildly then descended
and darkly consumed her. And the baby.
She began to cry softly. She was exhausted.
She was alone. But eventually she slept.
She couldn't speak to him of her night-time flight.
Their argument next morning was pointless somehow.

But there was more to bear.
Why did Tom say the imminent birth
of their first child was inconvenient that day,
if it happened as foretold
would probably be in the middle of an important meeting,
For him, for us. 'One I've planned for weeks.'

He came away to the hospital unwillingly,
fell in love with the small, creased baby face,
nursed the child with a tenderness so welcomed.
'I'm the first to hold him!' he proclaimed
Before you've even held him,' and she smiled at him.
'You're the first in the world, Tom.'
Because that's what he wanted to hear.
And he was pleased.

But even then, it wasn't Tom who fetched her
and the new baby from hospital.
Tom was caught up in more meetings.
Her father said 'Don't worry I'd be delighted.'
He didn't mind that he was mistaken for the father

of the little thing sleeping in her arms.
He laughed, 'an old ugly guy like me?'

'Just tell me this baby won't change anything,?'
Tom had demanded
that first afternoon a whole new uncertain role,
breasts engorged, hospital help behind her.
The baby cried, the crib was wet,
silent tears slid down her face,
She couldn't make them afternoon coffee, not right now…
Nervously feeding the wee intruder. Inadequate,
Now frightened baby cries…welling and welling
Eardrums ringing with it, fear rising, for the baby, for her,
Insufficient, inadequate, hopeless, repeating and repeating.

Tom left abruptly to find peace and coffee elsewhere.
But in the end he couldn't resist the baby
and the baby days were happy, he couldn't resist
the wonder of the growing thriving baby,
and even the idea of another
which blotted out the gaping hole
in their marriage, for a time.

On reflection she determined yet again,
she had somehow wounded Tom's manly pride
whatever that was. Early in the piece.
Early earnest discussions life, love, politics what?
Whatever she was, despite her love for him,
she had cut deep, with things she could not share
The shafts of poetry too deep to share
Spears and beams indestructible ever since childhood
Since first scribing magical words

impossible to explain to share, her selfhood
impossible to hear what would come,
his mocking of it not to be borne.
She had cut deep excluding him, cut deep
to where his true selfhood resided, must have,
yet had to be true to herself
so that she too, could survive, she reasoned
still after all this time shaky at the thought,
there being no middle ground for them.

Tempestuous sounds sexy and it was
for a time. Deep crazy fucking with Tom.
Long nights of it and deadly sleeping after,
A brief closeness following, a joy,
but not so close she would reveal things
like the night she took to the bathroom
to cry real tears of loss when a favourite poet died
known to her intimately on paper.
Tom would laugh at the very least
maybe remonstrate with her at the idea,
so she sat in bath weeping noiselessly
for lost words and worlds,
though the poet had lived a world away.
weeping as if for a dear friend,
maybe aware that so many former ideas
were dying, were already being left behind.
Tom's lovemaking that night was tender
as if he guessed something.

Illicit love

But she didn't really learn the utter bliss
sex could be, until later. Until Lucas.
Until slowness and delight.
Now a slow deliberate ecstatic holding back
for climax, for a better higher climax,
for the swooning that happens in the rise and fall
of lovemaking. The heat, the flagrance, the work of it,
going to an edge and teetering and teetering and not falling,
breathing and whispering and holding back and holding back
and then the urgency mounting, the upsurge
toward the paroxysm, now the feeling of
rising and grasping and reaching towards
breathlessness and deepness yet rising and rising
and this is ecstasy and knowing what it means
ecstasy, knowing what it is...
the flooding, the searing and the exaltation
of the shooting waves of exquisite orgasm.
As if giving up the idea of separation forever.

Lucas she thought, she understood why the penis might
be worshipped, penis and vagina both,
She thought of his, wantonly and desperately.
Lucas, svelte urbane and practised.
Soft heavy-lidded eyes, straight a fine nose, and a cleft chin,
Straight floppy hair to stroke
to sweep from his forehead to press lips to
Lucas who didn't understand he was saving her.
When is a betrayal not a betrayal?

Tom far away on a business trip,
golden nights with Lucas.
He'd been an accountant, now a lawyer,
his office in the city in an ultra-glamorous high rise
a small office on the unimportant side
of the swanky harbourside building, Sunday-empty.
 So they'd made love on the floor
and it seemed almost perfect.
Several times. Met for lunches in
ill-lit cafes where she found it difficult
not to touch his hand. Entangle him in some way,
encourage him to make promises.
none of which could be fulfilled.
Taking foolish chances.
Going home to his place,
the boldness the shabbiness of it.
His home suburban, disappointing,
tasteless artwork everywhere.
No! Horses galloping over a hill,
a single orchid on green steps,
A Pro Hart or two...
But she didn't really care. It wasn't for his taste...
They'd made love there once only
when his family was away (that was poor)
How could she have taken to the marital bed
without guilt. Maybe a little, but not enough.

They careened down the mad path of an affair.
From the first moment there was a breath of the farewell
in their lovemaking, this high pleasure could surely
not sustain. They were in a dream that for fruity moments
became reality. We are blessed she thought, when with him,

I am surely blessed, though it seemed impolite, offish,
to use this word for such an infidelity.
Blessed until she wasn't.

Rilke in Rodin's house, Paris

Henry, her student lover, gave her his precious
collector's book of poet Rainer Maria Rilke.
Rilke. Rilke. The name tinkling like a bell
Not that sad bell Keats talks of in his Nightingale poem,
tolling him back to his sad self…
No, the lighter Rilke bell,
spiritual love, erotic love and his
own persistent search for 'goodness.'

Years later in Paris with Tom, in the tearooms
at Rodin's house filled with his divine sculptures.
Rilke. A note about Rilke, his poems on their cafe table.
at Rodin's Paris house?
She couldn't explain to Tom the poems she'd shared with Henry
in student days then wheedling his precious Rilke book away
from him.

Now here in Paris the delight in
discovering that the poet, no less than Rilke himself
had once been Rodin's secretary. Rilke and Rodin.

This had been a good time with Tom.
Tom had smiled indulgently.
'You are so in love with their story…'
wondering out loud if he, the poet in residence,
had met the talented sculptor Camille Claudel
whose work is there too,
surely Rodin's inspiration for the sculpture

that knows no romantic equal,
the twining perfect sculpted pair
The Kiss?

Camille, Rodin's lover for many years,
Rodin who so admired her work.
Poor luckless talented Camille
sequestered in a mad house
when she became too outlandish,
a female sculptor who in one of her fits of temper
or was it despair, smashed most of her work
to bits
and in her 30 years in an asylum
refused release by her mother
and when her mother died,
refused release by her brother.
Camille Claudel whom Rodin had so admired.
Camille who never sculpted again
in her 30 year's incarceration.
How then did she pass her time?
We are wound around by stories
all the time she thought
even while regarding plants in a pond.

Savouring Rilke's name, and then another's,
Lou Andreas Salome rolling off the tongue
Telling an accommodating Tom this story too.
Lou Andreas Salome the older woman that Rilke had loved-
Essential cosmopolitan intellectual woman
Russian born. Bright and forward and unwomanly
for the time, who had loved Freud and Nietzsche.
was admired by Nietzsche, wrote on him and then

on Rilke after his early death.
Even now, the existential pulse
Rainer Maria Rilke, Lou Andreas Salome
Just saying names, hers and Rilke's
remembering them aloud,
stirring again the world of her early self-
the divine discovery of these impossibly far people
in love with art and poetry, impossibly clever
who lived their lives in it and by it
whom she loved and envied in equal measure.
Just naming them, just the idea of them
could make her tremble at the thought.

"Who, if I cried out, would hear me among the angels'
hierarchies? and even if one of them
pressed me against his heart: I would be consumed
in that overwhelming existence.
For beauty is nothing but the beginning of terror,
which we still are just able to endure,
and we are so awed because it serenely disdains to annihilate us.
Every angel is terrifying."

Rainer Maria Rilke, <u>Duino Elegies</u>

Going home

The pond stopped talking, just like that,
offering her anything.
and Evie was suddenly afraid again.
They had left her alone too long at the pond.
She shivered and gathered herself,
eyes up to the verandahh
and rose, uncramping her legs
and moving through the garden slowly
careful still of the webs criss-crossing the way
and yet uneasy.

When she walked up the stone steps and towards the door
she wondered why they'd not called out.
She was cold, it was late, edge of darkness even,
and the door swung open at her touch.
When she went inside the house
there was no one there after all;
no dinner warmth, people cooking
music of glasses clinking, murmur of voices,
mumblings of radio or TV or both,
rather a silence swept down the hall towards her.
Dear aunt and uncle, dearest Totti and Toby!
No one!
She could get into a panic about this.
No, she would not!
She'd stayed too long at the pond.
That was it and time had passed,
simple as that. Too much time.

Hours, weeks!
Maybe years.

She looked around her finding the familiar.
Ah yes! her paintings, but a favourite hanging crooked?
Totti was obsessive about straightening things.
'Totti,' she called her voice weak on the yellow air.
'Toby,' a lot louder, but to no avail.
The fancy bird cage rusted and empty, hanging
by the back door, waiting for first sun
The bleak memory.
The way Toby had sobbed at its death.
Canary Jack out of the cage early Saturday morning
The big man had stepped back
And each man kills the thing he loves
not seeing the little bird
pecking at crumbs on the floor.
Inconsolable. Totti had cried too
and neither had talked of its replacement
as neighbours had advised.
'Quicker the better too,' as if there could be another...
Just the empty cage. And Toby's forever guilt.

Ah her books, comforting shelves of them!
And screeds of her writing piled up on the desk,
familiar names, was she recording the pond?
But were they cobwebs in the corner?
and at one window some broken glass.
Heart stop pounding, breathe slowly, slowly.
There never had been anyone else here?
Just her?
Morpheus shaping them into existence.

Maybe it was a dream she had of those
dear folks from the farm of her childhood
deep in the winter rain's bright green or
sometimes dusty yellow part of
interior inland country up north in New South Wales,
the ample wooden farmhouse with its views
of distant forests and old volcanic peaks
that always seemed a refuge. Country house away,
home-made everything. She remembered sharply
what a refuge after her mother died, the baby died,
her marriage broke and she had broken too,
in so many ways.

Maybe she dreamed them here in the city
whose hands reached out to comfort her, hold her
Maybe it was part of her depressions, the madness.
Phantoms.
But no, there were photos Totti and Toby
their dear particular and wholesome faces
so black and so white and proper in their studio record
of their war time marriage. The plain white flowing dress,
the crimped hair under the small beflowered veil.
Toby uncomfortable in bow tie but handsome
and upright, and then those silver framed photos,
both so smiling in the faded colours of their garden.

And a sudden rush of death memories so clear.
Toby's death first, the terrible slow way he descended
complainingly into ill-health
and the merciful fast way that pneumonia took him,
hastened further in the end the family doctor attending.

Not too much later, was it only months, Totti's going.
That sudden little cry 'Oh!' and that's all
 before she fell forward, head on the table,
 amid the tea things, her cup spilling,
arms hanging limply.
She had known at once Totti was dead.
Evie gave a cry of pain now, as if they were
both Toby and Totti, quite recent bereavements.
They said you don't call it madness these days,
depression, delusions, paranoia, whatever.

Her mental state

Evie had called it her 'madness' a now unfashionable word
and feared it more than any single thing.
Her particular affliction.
It was after the baby died unreasonably quickly
of a perfectly curable ailment, the madness began.
The walking began as if she could outwalk the thing.
They told her they were panic attacks but panic
is sharp and sudden in her mind.
This feeling is more about dread,
a rising fear, a rising horror, always slowly rising,
that can't be fully named let alone understood.

That manic pacing and doing things,
folding things like paper or washing, folding smaller
and neater than ever before, folding, folding,
and sorting things like tumbled drawers
folding and sorting things might begin to outstrip
the feeling, weigh it down, keep it in place
by the doing, the constant doing.

Kindness of people around her,
diversions books, TV shows, normal conversations.
But she learned sitting too long was dangerous,
stillness could be deathly, better to stand,
if someone wanted to talk to her,
if someone drew up a chair to be near her,
she had to stand behind her own chair
to be able to go on, (escape made easy perhaps?)

to talk to her friend or whoever. They'd have to understand.
The bell jar thing, the daunting separation.
She had to stand and then she had to walk away,
leave the madness in the room, behind the chair, wherever
as if it had a will of its own with her.
And she had a chance, a slim one but a chance
to walk it down, at least that!
If she walked and walked. If she kept moving.
These feelings will subside she was promised
with the right drugs and time, and it did, or seemed to.

She wrote a poem about it ,
inspired by Emily Dickinson's funeral poem
and the psychologist asked could she keep a copy.
Even though she thought it inept it comforted her
that something had come out of months of trembling
at the brink, of something prodding and burrowing
ready to seep in and sweep her away.

I felt the dread, an ocean of dread...
It shatters my knowing, drives a spear through my soul
I cannot outwit it, whatever I'm told.

I felt the dread, I am on evil's ledge
Precipitous hand, I am over an edge.
When grey mist starts shifting, the blessed relief
The right to stay still, to rest, even sleep.

But always those remnants awry on the breeze
The cold realisation, tenacious strands tease.
An ocean of dread, might lap in my head
Might reach out to take me, wherever I've fled.'

Maybe the empty house,
the expectation of the loving pair
was a dream invented for her comfort?
Being with them here the loving pair,
the oh so ordinary familiar everyday pair
rich in something missing in her life,
torn awry as it felt.
Some innocence, some damnable wisdom it seemed.
Scolding each other continuously
but each folding into the other
even in familiar disagreements about the world,
the garden, the glasses moved, the horses slavishly followed,
as she had folded into someone, long ago.

Tom and the deeply tender times of their marriage
She was finding harder to ignore, somehow accosted by them.
Tom a seaside person, in the water making her a sea person,
and the easy embrace in the deep, tangling round each other
eyes only for each other in that lulling place.
Quixotic, quick, a mystery man.
Ten years of marriage and yet not an inkling really
of what drove this man, what really tempered him.
The fierce joy and the fierce rage...
and then thinking back, his inconsistencies and yes
his cruelties seemed to outweigh the other?
And it was easy to feel anger! A sense of so much lost time.
But what of her weaknesses, her own failure to disengage?

Trying to understand the sadness
that would come unbidden to sit beside you,
warning you of its excess, the chasm to come.

Petite cracks in it like a fine old vase
crazed they called it but quietly so-
quietly to sit by you and wait.
At first like a dog lying at your feet,
no, more a cat springing to you lap
and you could only soothe it for a while.
But then it's neither cat nor dog
nor anything understandable,
more a monster thing taking over
wracking, defiant and cruel
a cataclysm about to overtake,
a bending over with the weight of it,
death in the air, but worse than death
a drilling down on your soul,
the uselessness of tears,
rather a tearing at your core, upheaval in the blood
your inner self to shreds now a dogged thing inside.

She heard her own breath quicken at these thoughts
And calmed herself by deliberate slow even breaths.
That was all in the past, surely. Only wraiths now,
Meeting her memories as she had been, as she was,
this was surely a new strength?

Blue, Blue Mountains and Rob

The tranche of memories entangling her now,
confusing and yet sometimes enlivening.
And next day at the pond allowing it again.
They took one journey together, one only
Out of Sydney. She and Rob
and the end of things for them.

Rob Connor didn't really fancy leaving the city.
'Ever,' he said. Blue Mountains or not.
'I'm like the filmmaker Woody Allen,
who always said it makes him nervous,
pastoral scenes and trees, so many!
But she had cajoled and he had agreed.
Well, who doesn't like a train trip?
They were at the *Poet and Peasant.*
The old joke again, it still made her laugh,
'I'm the peasant...
 where she read her poetry to him.
And he clasped her hand in his,
'And you're truly the poet, darling. You really are a poet!'
His admiration making her tremble.
The only person who would ever say that!
The only person in the world.
Sharing a pasta, sharing a glass of wine.
Short of money. Her allowance almost gone.
And poetry. Hers and then the Rilke he said he loved.
He produced some crumpled paper and smoothed it.

We need in love to practice only this: letting each other go.
For holding on comes easily; we do not need to learn it.
She wasn't sure of that one and sipped the wine
But liked the next he read
Find out the reason that commands you to write
See whether it has spread its roots
in the very depth of your heart,
Confess to yourself you would rather have to die
if you were forbidden to write.
Oh yes she told him she understood that!
He wrote to young poets, one in particular
I must give you that book!
Rob seemed more than usually happy and she dared ask
something she'd been thinking about for weeks,
'Should we go away from the city. Just for a day?'
'Away?' he seemed surprised.
But away to a favourite place.
'The Blue Mountains, part of my childhood. Together?'
He took the remainder of the wine and smiled at her.
'Who doesn't like a train trip?' As if he had a car and a choice.
Maybe not even the train fare?

Some places matter in your life and all your life
she told him. And this is one for me.
Evie remembered her father in his dying days
wanting to come to this very place, to his sister
and to the valley of his early manhood.
as his strength fled him. To fly to them.
Places as much as people.
Your former self somehow confirmed.
Blue Mountains and the mysterious grandmother
In the old verandahh-ed homestead,

Proud, unbending with her jabbing wit
her fair share of hardship, perhaps not fair,
her vanity and loathing of her own old age,
only her dark eyes retaining their striking beauty
despite the fine sagging lines around them.
Her resoluteness and her wondrous cooking,
deft hands rolling out more marvels-
her old fuel ovens that gave up such an aroma
along with the splinters of wood, red hot flames
'yet cooking,' as she explained, 'to perfection.'
Pies and scones by the dozens for her tearooms
and for a little girl, for Evie,
their ordinary perfection she managed with ease.

What is the magnetism of a place
that's been part of a childhood?
the inexplicable call to return, to re-view
things as they were, your former self
to see your other self.
Just yourself?
With plaits and protruding front teeth,
with a sense of wonder and scribblings kept
in exercise books, secret, at a time
when paper was revered and even saved.
What of her in me she wondered,
any of them?
But in the end there is no going back
though something surely smoulders.
For her, it was the Blue Mountains and a grandmother
she still wanted to speak of...

Blue Mountains mornings of her childhood

and the rising up of the valley,
grasses heavy yet with dew,
paddocks wetly stretching to rainforest edge
and eyes drawn to that manmade castle
a hotel, on a yellow cliff, the glorious Hydro Majestic,
majestic and unreachable to childish eyes,
valley rimmed with eucalypt trees
with broken yellow sandstone bulwarks,
thousands of years of rocks and caves
small waterfalls and curving creeks
fires being lit, tools fashioned,
engravings etched into in solid rock
family life, tribal stories played out.
'They were called the Gundungorra,'
she explained
and yes she'd written a poem about them
after trekking to a place deep in the valley
there mysteriously called Mermaids' Cave.
'We should go there too, this place
where she'd imagined Gundungorra folk
bathing and fishing and playing
with not a sight of a mermaid!
She'd told Rob all of this on the train.
Life played out, remnants now
Megalong magic, 'megalong' a word that meant
Valley-under-the rock, so suited.

Train journey away

Central Railway Station and Rob that day.
And Central of the high domed roof
and the persistent birds across the glass,
of the expectant engine line-up.
The gritty welcome smell of childhood
rising up all round her, of asphalt!
Familiar platforms, generous with slatted wood seats,
cottage green and cream wood awnings
and the hurrying figures,
or the stray leaners and lookers.
She found he prided himself on last minute,
she pretending they were a regular couple,
walking very close to him.
Not that he seemed to mind.
for Rob took her hand in his own.
On the train he began telling her
of what he'd been reading
of Seneca a philosopher she didn't know,
but wanted to know, Rob!
'So bloody wise this guy, Evie
Had to kill himself on Nero's orders
and killed himself three times!'
'Whaaat?' she laughed.
'Before it worked.
Sad, first time like Socrates
a goblet of hemlock but his didn't work
then by cutting his veins but Nero's soldiers
got impatient as he wasn't dying fast enough

old veins don't bleed as readily as younger ones,
more vein-letting and immersion in a warm bath
to bleed more freely...and that did it.
But he was brave to the end.'

Accept whatever happens as per Seneca.
 He maintains we're answerable for our own unhappiness
'Suffering is often more in our minds than in reality'
She didn't like to say that she disagreed.
That what you were most afraid of
she believed would more than likely come to pass!

 Rob read out more in declaratory tone,
 'Never act on the basis of anger. Be mindful of triggers
make 'paths' with conscious purpose.'
Here's a good bit Evie!
'Limit association with the crowd.
Big crowds are not good in fact they hold you back
Retire into yourself so that you know yourself all the better
Focus on what you do best'
To find purpose. And so on...'

He loved being teacherly to her which was
good in one way but also a worry.
Did he think she was 12 when she was almost 20!
She listened to this impossible list.
Loved hearing things philosophical
but should she admit to him
that she'd only read Will Durant's *Story of Philosophy*
a thickish popular paperback that had intrigued her,
 but that all her understanding of great thinkers
actually resided in Durant's potted accounts.

It was surely all too hard to be that Seneca kind of person
but she felt brave and thoughtful sitting so close to him.

They were together on a train at her behest too,
and travelling back into her childhood.
He'd listened intently to some of her story.
And now they were silent.
Bursts of wattle track-side
from grey green bush to lemon yellow
like a continuous bobbing garland.

'Ain't nature grand,' he said spoiling it just a little.
They were plunging into a tunnel.
Darkness and the magnified sound of the train
moments on end so she reached for his hand,
then hurtling out into light, bushland falling away
to a village glimpsed for short moments.
'What do you make of it all, eh little Evie?'
Taking out a cigarette to tap on the pack,
making that smoke filled with cloves and other
dream around the carriage satisfyingly.
She wanted to say something deep and thoughtful
but 'I see light at the end of the tunnel,' came to mind
And she started smiling.
And when she told him he laughed.

Confession

As they climbed upwards towards Katoomba
'Listen pet, something I want to tell you.
Today while we're here.'
Making her heart constrict. 'What?'
His face suddenly altogether too serious.
'I'm going away soon and before I do,
I want to tell you something important.'
'We are away,' she said calmly, 'Really away!'
She didn't quite believe him about going away
as the bush sped by
greener and thicker than she remembered,
and he was warm and languid right beside her.
This is Away!

She could see his more solemn mood dissolve
as she kissed his cheek over and over,
and then his lips when he turned to her, 'Away!'
Making him smile and making her repeat it.
'Not going anywhere.'
But it was the day something unfolded,
something he had to say
that changed things and her idea of him altogether.
Wasn't it? Didn't it?

Well out with it or let it remain forever buried.
Deep in the interlacing tree roots of the valley
in that clearing where they made love
or sunken here in the reflecting pond, Evie thought,

like her aunt's unsuccessful water lily pots.
But her search was indeterminate.
A series of images of them together
and then their love-making
But something else unnerving there, yes?
That simply 'was' as blue, blue mountains engulfed them..

A whole day in the old-fashioned places,
Katoomba round and about,
with its old-so-old craggy cliffs
with its tea and scones and mountain devils,
very few now for sale. She told Rob
of the protected plant, the devil, a horned seed pod
that women of the mountains
dressed in a bright red capes
using shearing scissors to make them
attaching red pipe cleaners limbs
and selling the devils to all comers.
until there was concern
that the Proteaceae shrub would disappear
altogether and devils with it.

They held hands at the Three Sisters
kissed at the ancient tearooms
made love on the valley floor
rode up in the terrifying steep mountain train
through a mountain mist.
'My life's in the mist,' he said, 'in and out!'
Caressing her face, her hand, her neck.
When he was melancholy like this she loved him
more than ever, wanted to lift him bodily out of the mist
to be beside her. Allow him to feel happy as she was!

That happiness that throbbed so unreasonably
right through her in his company.
Let's walk to them,' she said.
And they took the walk out there
To the three stout but surely crumbling sisters.
Read the sign out loud.

*Pass through the archway, next to the Echo Point Visitor Centre,
and you'll soon be surrounded by soaring eucalypt forest, bird calls
and fresh mountain air. Keep an eye out for the superb lyrebird and
crimson rosellas as you walk the gently sloping path for 400m to
Oreades lookout.*

Leaning on the rusting wire fence
'Tempting fate,' he said, testing it.
The blue not so much in shades
as in deepening layers
'A going outness Rob,
sublime, all the way to Mt Solitary'.
'Solitary like me,' he said.
Why did it always come back to him
and why did she never question it?
as if his maturity of 5 years or 6 years
gave him centre stage rights perhaps.

Ecstasy

'Solitary? Not right now,' she said leaning against him.
feeling peculiarly proprietal right then.
'I remember as a child,' now she was now claiming centre stage,
'the first time I felt 'ecstasy' out in nature.
No, don't laugh, I did.'
'Go on,' her smiled at her and she plunged on
filled with the surprise of it.

'Dad took us out to a vantage point
somewhere near here. Sublime Point and it was!
It took just about a day to drive up here
from Sydney then. Mostly winding roads,
in a borrowed car, our mother pointing out things
all the way, like the tree that the three explorers marked
as first men over the Blue Mountains.
But our Dad said of course they were not the first!
First people lived here for aeons. Crossed over easily.
'Sublime Point. Sublime!' she was quiet, a moment.
'Go on,' Rob said.

Dad took us down a rough bush track.
In a clearing our mother stopped
settling in the strange little grotto-like
cement house that looked as if it had been
built by goblins for elves.
with its shells and pebbles packed neatly.
'Don't take them close to edge,' our mother said
'I'll follow on.'

'All this is coming back right now, Rob.
Do you really want to hear?'
'Ecstasy,' he reminded her.
'We ran down that track ,
my brother and my sometime friend Francie
a slither, a glimpse of what lay ahead
but not expecting the sight, the utter grandeur!

Catching sight of that spectacle, Rob
the view that dropped and soared
at the same time, the one that drew the breath
out of you for moments on end,
from hills to mountain crags,
I wanted to run right to edge and yell out
'Beauty! Beauty!' As if I'd just discovered its meaning
Its true meaning. And I felt it. An ecstasy!'

She knew her face must have been flushed
with the telling as she turned to him.
'I love you so much,' Rob said quietly
taking her hand and bending forward
to kiss it.
No, Evie, he didn't say that, she reminded herself.
He never actually said that he loved her, ever.

She stared down at the nearby beauty of the pond surface,
this morning boasting a water lily not yet unfurled.
She knew she had just wanted him to- it was the moment,
Rob didn't speak at all, but he did take her hand.
And then they stood silently looking out at a vista
that spread hills apart and let torrents run through it and over it.

At the same time, a landscape of blues and greens
so many soft shades of blue all the way
to the edge of the world,
the absolute blanket of deep green at their feet
and they, succumbing to the superb astonishing hues
as hundreds, thousands had done before them,
hues enfolding them. Blue, blue mountains.

A jubilant little wind played a kind of
bush tune for them then
sighing breathy and silvery sounds,
rock sounds, trees quietly talking,
sounds she knew and did not know.
'Music of the mountains,' she murmured.
She felt right now they were experiencing
bliss, like at Sublime Point but different,
being with him, with Rob,
the immensity and now the striking intimacy.

Making love

She and Rob Connor were away,
'Away,' she kept thinking, 'We're away!'
as if in another world that was to be fully theirs.
almost inconceivable,
not in a coffee shop
or a park, in a laneway,
a theatre foyer, or a friend's flat.
Or even a friend's hallway.
Away.
They were sitting a little apart,
hot and tired after a long descent
snaking twirling down a natural stony track
into a ferny glade the bottom of this wide valley.
Huge boulders had tumbled down here
from those looming and encircling cliffs
so long ago; boulders not perching
as much as inhabiting with their fringes of ferns
and their now svelte stone bodies moss covered
and leaf littered.

Rob pulled her towards him and
behind the largest of one of these boulders
off track and secluded,
to be alone. He spread his coat
'Gallant you see!' he said to her.
'down in the green valley...'
'Jamison Valley,' she told him,
almost feeling shy at being so hidden away

in this easily lying down place.
'Renamed by Lachlan Macquarie,'
as if that fact were important.
'I'd say the Evie Valley today,'
as he drew her down beside him.

It was green and dense, damp with aromatic foliage,
'in our own dream-like Shakespeare's midsummer,'
Rob began
I know a bank where the wild thyme blows,
Where oxlips and the nodding violet grows,
Quite over-canopied with luscious woodbine,
With sweet musk-roses and with eglantine.
Gorgeous well-worn words and she didn't contradict him,
though waratahs bloomed all around them
and bottlebrush, myrtles and bush grasses.
Over-canopied a perfect description
for the frieze of gum leaves hanging above them,
the damp fernery all around
strong eucalypt and other scents all around them
and some hard things
a few twigs and pods tunnelling into her shoulder.
'Aromata,' she murmured suffused by so many bush smells
and his closeness.

Lingering kisses, desultory talk, then
an amazing fulfilling silence between them.
'Evie,' rolling over and closer beside her
the look of purpose was unmistakable.

The urge unmistakable. A blissful compulsion.
'Evie,' that tender yet almost anguished expression
No, a pleading expression,
'You're too young to be with me. This is...
And her smiling anticipation. 'Yes.'
Then not so desultory kisses and no more words.
Their concentration on finding each others' bodies
in swathes of clothing. Getting rid of some of them.
Not even awkward but funny, eager, the grappling
with buttons and zippers, shirt sleeves
wriggling and laughing, and more kisses.
The dim realisation of his fumbling for a condom
and then sumptuous feeling of his naked flesh,
her flesh against his softness
how could such a big man feel so soft?
her face buried in his too big shoulder
and the sensuous smell of him,
of soap and sweat and the lingering clove smell
still in his hair.
The weight, now a hard weight upon her
'Evie, Evie' and then
his sudden silence, deep breaths,
the driving force of it unstoppable
stronger, deeper, in and inside her
the pain, the deep pleasure,
and the pain inside her
great juddering spasms of it and then
the crying and the relief and the feeling of
some sort of summation and delight.
Some deep fathomable pleasure
The continuing spasms and twinges of it
when he'd come, that seemed to pulse

right through her vagina and her abdomen
even her belly, maybe her ovaries she thought,
as if new parts of her body discovered
New pleasures, the pleasure of pleasures.
Repeating his name as if a mantra.

The blissful feeling of lying together
in their green mansions, their bush mansion
looking up into swirling branches above,
his arm round her now resting against his warmth
'Darling' and 'are you all right?'
'Mmm,' she couldn't express the kind of soaring gladness
 of now, the wonder of the body, the joy.

They lay quietly and she saw he'd closed his eyes.
She looked up into clusters of leaves, up and up tree trunks,
dangling swathes of bark, so many stippled tree trunks
as she inhaled the dank earth.
'Do you ever imagine underneath us? she asked him.
'I mean the lacing together of all these tree roots
right under our bodies. And how in love with each other
they'd have to be to survive. So interconnected.'
'No!' he said. 'Must say I don't!'
'Life!' she said touching his face, his lips.
'More and more life!
'Not right now,' he said, disengaging
sitting up, discarding the condom
pulling up trousers, reaching for his shirt.
Kisses in between but a new intent.

She didn't ever want to leave, she thought
reluctantly pulling on her clothes,

but the mountain afternoon cold was already
slicing into the dappled sunlight
and though he smiled at her she sensed
his mood change as he sat up
finding a cigarette and lighter
and puffing at it, thoughtful now.

Serious stuff

'I know I have to tell you Evie, you of all people.'
He'd hugged her to him a moment,
'something important to tell you,' in low tones
but not as a lover might speak now
and she knew instinctively
it was not something she wanted to hear.
'Not now,' was all she said.
A scuttling frilled-necked lizard
was threading its way toward them,
ponderous with its flickering skin and tongue
'No,' she said as if a premonition, scaring it away
With a wave of her hand. 'No!'
'Do not!' But he was saying something to her.
She thought she'd heard the word murder
and she could see the coming tears
in his eyes, and she could hear herself,
'No, Rob don't, not now.'
As if it might end everything
that was not even properly begun.
'Tortured me a long time!
and you're the one. Of course you are!
That's why we met in the first place
I'm sure of it!' As if fate had played a part.
As if she alone could conjure up forgiveness?

'You're the one who can bear it!'
And he was shaking,
those big manly shoulders shaking.

She had heard the word though,
and hurled it away from her,
refused it. 'It's all right Rob!
You don't have to say any more. I understand.'
Soothing him then until he was still.
'I've needed to tell someone for years,' he said
Suddenly she felt the weight of it. But why me?
At the unfairness of spoiling things like this,
'No one to confide in Rob- your family?'
A grim little laugh...
Family when he seemed so footloose.
Family might pinion you but it can mind you too.
Funny that she was thinking that right now.

Liaisons in a lifetime
shaping a lifetime
measuring a lifetime?
Rob Connor why wonder about him,
disappeared long since.
But still she wondered
why had he come and gone so memorably
And now, she wondered again?

She would never know fully of some dark past,
of his character true self if there's such a thing.
A remittance man, a criminal, a 'bounder'
A con man, a dreamer, a charmer,
What of it? Or just someone tarrying in Sydney
who longed for another life too?
Reece told her Rob had gone to live in Ireland,
permanently, he said with a wry smile, an uncle...
a well-off uncle and living alone

and more or less begging him to come.
True or false he'd packed his bags
Rob Connor and he'd gone.
Ah yes! Oscar Wilde returns...
She'd had enough rethinking of Rob Connor
Enough now!

And yet she just knew she should stay here
at the pond, in the garden, gathering
assembling, concentrating,
until it worked itself out,
until she worked herself out,
and Rob's part in it?
treading on eggshells, no, at times
more like leaping across shattered glass.

Part 7
Normandy, France to Sydney Again

*'And something settled on her like
the sable dusk settles'*

With Tom in Normandy

She was still 'gleaning,' staying here.
Garnering like the poor in the Bible
allowed to wander through the harvested fields
to garner, collect whatever if any is left,
gleaning from the garden,
right here by the pond, day after day
hour after hour,
thought after tumbling thought...

The wind was blowing quite wilfully
through the top of the tangled garden,
palms bending and whipping at the damp air,
fronds and sheaves and pods flying-
She looked around her
imagining all this gone. Then up at the house.
This place, this familiar beloved place...
Tom had never seen this place. Tom...

The last holiday with her husband
with Tom, in the small French chateau
last times, last moments, last...
In the north of Normandy not far from Paris
near Ornay-sur-Odon, a small village
razed during World War 2, but for the miracle
church wall and spire left intact and inspiring
a rebuild of the whole town,
comforting but somehow disturbingly new
in a Europe prized for its history, its past,

they said, finding the coffee shop that was to be theirs,
whose window was bordered with tiny coloured flags
of all nations. Of all allied nations that is.

Soon saw their flag and the words of thanks
to the Allies. 'Australian flag there too.
Ever grateful,' Tom remarked
not untouched by the tribute
to the long dead. She told him
as she had tried to, before
that she had a relative buried in Belgium
and he said he probably did too.
'All those poor bloody country lads thinking
Europe would be a great adventure.'
She'd just finished the novel *Birdsong*
and said he should read it
but the disapproving line of his lips
said she should stop making suggestions
about Tom's reading matter.

After ancient villages of stone and cobbled streets,
with their medieval timbered and half-timbered houses
with their apple cider presses and brimming flowerpots
stolid red outside the odd stone houses with blue shutters
down charming country roads
brakes in the high hedgerows
long moments, fields of shaggy grass
thick with purple thistles, studded with
primroses and oxslip, wood anemones and bluebells
and the famous black and white cattle
unperturbed by passers by
exploring this part of Normandy,

ever to remain their part of Normandy
in the warmth of late summer.

The odd farmhouse and yes,
map-wrangling and raised voices
on and on down flowery lanes
and yes, finally there it was
a handsome stone chateau
with a three hundred year history,
Just like that!
They were being *given* a chateau, 'A small one
and as long as you need...'

Tom's new English friend
antique dealer Charles had begun its restoration
with gusto. 'But you know,' had said shrugging,
'we've had it two years already, hardly go there now,
so have it long as you like!'

In the ruined chateau,
in the ruined marriage

A chateau with its lovely stone façade,
and its ruined out-buildings,
with its serious need of repair
yet still habitable, very pleasantly so,
except one room in the west wing
where annoyingly the roof was actually caving in,
he'd get it 'seen to next visit
but just avoid that end of the place...'

The chateau all its French charm.
seemed filmic and dreamlike
roof falling in or no
as if in a dream, making the dream,
a feeling that persisted all that extraordinary stay.
'Collecting French antiques, perfect place
To store then ship them! Charles had said,
'You should do it too. Money to be made, Tom!'

Little bits of its history they found
in old newspapers flung on a dusty table
Goes back a bit. Waterloo!
The home of the Marquis de Grouchy the general
who failed to reply to Napoleon's request
taking his horses, his men to another smaller battle
and arriving too late, Waterloo already lost,
the English and Prussian troops already victorious...
Wellington of course she'd heard of, but this other

General Blücher with his 30,000 Prussian troops?
Surely, a shared victory? No mention of?
'So much for our 1960's text books,' Tom said

Every room a depository of Charles'
collected treasures.
Tom and Evie took days to explore.
The long ballroom wiÜth its piled-up tables
and elegant chairs, several sets,
with its paintings, sideboards and bookshelves,
its marble clocks, propped mirrors
and scattered armoires,
with its several at least Ducati motorbikes.

A hustle of furniture on dusty black and white marble floor.
One corner with its ceiling to floor french windows
letting in dusty streams of light, soft and muted
and quite unlike the verve of the light of home.
She notices and remarks the light of Europe
can flood the place but somehow gently.

Bookcases, the lure and the trap of
such a wealth of old books, French and English
An early Alice she was tempted to take,
she'd make an offer on it, but thoughtfully put it back.
Enough of collecting and collecting...

To delve through leather bound French volumes
and heavy folders, bound folios and albums,
touch the keys of two, three elderly Olivetti typewriters
slung around on small tables,
and a serious collection of tin model cars.

Tom said they were all sports cars and she wondered
about the boy in Tom's collector friend,
cars all set about more carefully here, lined up
on a once shining wooden sideboard.

Back through the cluttered ballroom
and trying to imagine the time
before Waterloo, the 1800s and the life here...
live orchestras, live dancers, live servants, live partygoers
the terrace filled with the elite of Normandy
the owner, the Marquis, plump and gouty, surveying it all!
Master of all the chateau, the stables, the gardens
and the summer houses, a celebratory place
until Napoleon's loss at Waterloo!

But the here and now, the broken-downness
was for them more wonderful. Being here!
On the other side of the handsome stone facade
the long hallways hung with dank tapestries,
the bathroom of the still life windows
and out-of-keeping bunched blue floral curtains,
and its deep bath for lying soaking, dreaming,
and almost unbelieving,
the expansive view of green fields beyond;
the odd passers by in the shape of horses' heads,
horses parading past the bathroom window
almost incredulous that
this was possible and yet here they were
and it was theirs, not only the bathroom with a view,
all of it, a house of dreams...tattered and quite perfect.

The bedroom they claimed, the only room quite restored
with those two French windows, yet
a defiant English décor, pretty and rosy,
other bedrooms each with a hue of dilapidation,
the pretty stairwell hung with gold-framed paintings,
first landing, some portraits unremarkable
two handsome duck paintings and
a landscape of black and white cows.
Second landing more portraits,
one a nun, a lithograph, two.
Landscapes with hay ricks and a night painting
too dark to make much out but a beginning sun
on a deep navy horizon,
all of it to explore…and theirs.

Their junk filled ballroom, the deteriorating library
and the over-stuffed dining room, three or was it four
more tables haphazard with vases, and clocks
brass candlesticks, and then a room, a floor strewn
transistor radios of every shape and size.
All this would take days to see
let alone the time to explore the depths of the cellar.
'Let's make a morning of it.'
and venturing further up into the attics
'Let's make an afternoon of it.
and take our time along the widow's walk'.

It was the time of the chateau
of our chateau she thought
of exploration delightful.
It was a time of French countryside,
country roads with flowers by maize fields

poppies, nettles and purple coneflowers
with their Mary shrines studded along the way;
of nearby villages and their patisseries
of cafes and haberdashery shops, unique shops
hard to label
like the shop that sold pancakes, wine and coffee
and books but had an old-fashioned working organ,
that almost but not quite, blocked the entrance way,
and if you could get by it you could have a soufflé
perfect! if you have the time. And they did.

The odd small markets selling disparate things;
a jar of marvellous old buttons,
celluloid, Bakelite and pearl and china,
from jackets and dresses to soldier uniforms unsorted,
old instruments, from farm tools, a scythe,
a winnowing frame to battered trumpets.

And the market towns with largesse to spare;
lacework, carpets, tablecloths, curious chairs
farmhouse chairs, grand chairs, baby chairs.
And one miraculous morning
Evie had said it was miraculous for this discovery
and Tom had agreed, was a whole table of
documents in fine hand writing marked 1703,
a notary's lists. They bought several sheets
and a folder to carry precious booty. 1703!
Australia had not been invaded and colonized yet,
Europe still sailing ships and months away.
Maybe the Dutch but not the English sailing ships,
not the English for sure.

Unbelievable! Unimaginable!
And pored over them that night
with awkward translation
of copperplate handwriting
almost swooning over signatures
with flourishes magnificent
so many curls and embellishments!
and swashbuckling underlinings.
Agreeing it was agreeable indeed
to be bringing these European treasures
back to Australia, as agreeable
as bringing French furniture!

'Today I have been happy'

The pleasure was in the quietness and the aloneness
and the need of each other's company,
and outside in the natural world
the ease of their conjoint-ness.
So many pleasurable homecomings
to this ridiculous castle all theirs.
It was the time of an uncommon tenderness...
Things, things, the chateau full of things
But not things that owned them.

In her notebook she found her mother's card
she had once sent the card with portrait of
the poet, Rupert Brook, line drawn
and the poem, *Today I have been happy*
 and why was this card with her still?
To spur another poetic memory- a poem,
These I have loved:

Then, the cool kindliness of sheets, that soon
Smooth away trouble; and the rough male kiss
Of blankets; grainy wood; live hair that is
Shining and free; blue-massing clouds; the keen
Unpassioned beauty of a great machine;
The benison of hot water; furs to touch;
The good smell of old clothes; and other such—
The comfortable smell of friendly fingers,
Hair's fragrance, and the musty reek that lingers
About dead leaves and last year's ferns.

                    Dear names,
And a thousand other throng to me!

And she could hear only her mother's voice
whenever she read them - those dear names...
Lovely to read aloud
because she had to be calm to read
to find, a reasonable loving mother.
The one she should have been all her life long.

The day she and Tom had found cassettes in the chateau
all over the floor of what had once been a dining room
and could choose from an assortment of plastic transistor players
to hear from the random music dumped here.
There weren't French composers, German or European at all.
In the dusty pile an old Elvis Presley that Tom soon clicked to life
sensuous, breathy and sweetly familiar.
'And shall we dance?'
And they did around the laden table
in between the scattered players,
easy in each other's arms,
and so much was swept away with the music
being held by Tom like this
and not quite knowing why,
it was an ending of sorts...
but this time a beautiful ending.
Love me tender
Love me true
All my dreams fulfill....
Whole moments in that sway
where the first tumult of their relationship
the first sweetness and expectation
even the wildness, the longing re-membered
and some sort of sexual reconciliation
when his arms held her tight, almost as it had been...

That night he awoke in a fever
and she fetched a cold cloth
and aspirins and they talked as the dawn painted
an excessively beautiful French picture
through long windows nearby
and when he slept she felt the sadness invading
and left the bed and walked downstairs
glad of the thudding feet of several horses
already outside, sometime visitors
those young horses that roamed freely,
glad to watch them
approach their broad front stairs
and bank of long glass doors bereft of paint
but handsome still,
and then to pass by to more favoured
sweeter grasses of the untouched fields
at the back of the chateau
before it became forest again.

Four of them suddenly appearing,
dark horses she smiled, all four.
Three with a blaze of white
down handsome long faces,
one mother and her foal keeping close
all aware of the other. A pack? No herd
Mob? Herd, wasn't it for horses.
Short stocky horses, thickish legs
rough coats and uncombed manes,
yet well fed and calm, and free to wander.
She wondered a special Norman breed.
A small draught horse maybe...

She crossed the threshold to follow their path,
saw them pausing in the tangle
of tumbled down walled garden
to feed and nuzzle each other and then
unhurriedly move on.
A sense of proprietorship, that's what it was,
just as she and Tom had here
immediately after arrival in a strange place
in a strange land. Like entering a painting, a photograph,
and finding a strength in being united there.

'Met his Waterloo,' she mused finding an old paper
with more history of the place its original owner.
Curious. 'Waterloo, ending 23 years of war,
which must have been...'
Here in the depth of historic events and yet
feeling remarkably Australian in so many ways,
Regarding it all through the lens
of their habitual distance from Europe
as if again and again as they'd said
the feeling of being in a play, in a film!
They said they'd both felt it. As they said
they didn't want to leave and she added,
'not even for Paris.'

Caught out of time,
trapped in a cocoon of place
where dreams were in the making
and they knew it
and time to be considered in different ways.
Each day a kind of loitering and lingering,

shorter trips to nearby villages
and mediaeval towns
Today I have been happy...all the day

'We should go to Bayeaux,' Tom had said a few times
as they wandered through another village.
'Yes, we should,' she agreed.
He had become her friend again.
Already on the way to England he had relaxed,
by France he had changed,
more to the point, she became his friend, too
That was the crying shame of it,
just ridiculous simple pleasure
as it was in the beginning is now and
ever shall be, should be,
a love that tolled its own bell, immutably
as it was, is now, and ever shall be, love without end.
She remembered the words
The night they danced to the breathy deep voice
through the litter of the dining room
– a love that could never be meaningless
or without end,
and where she saw the end of things.

For the love of poetry,
for the love of Evie?

And now fonder memories surged across the pond
Tom overwhelming...
Remember how he'd driven her twice
that extended time they'd stayed in England,
driven all the way across Wales to the Boat House,
because first visit she'd been devastated
that Dylan Thomas's eggshell house
blues and greens and a sweeping sea
(that's the way she remembered it)
poised clifftop above the sweeping estuary
was *Closed to Visitors Today*.

Excluded! And no way she could stand at his poet's desk,
gaze at the view of the perilous incoming tide
and see it as he had seen it. So downcast
that next day Tom had taken her all the way across again
from the Forest of Dean to Laugharne,
all the way to the swirling estuary he drove
uncomplainingly, just to please her poetry obsession.

And Evie has sat at the desk of Dylan Thomas himself!
In the egg shell house with its swirling tides around it,
and seen the scrawl of 'bible-black' words
in his poet's hand and photographs and other
and lingered, as if touching the hem of his genius
one might be imbued with a speck of something,

dust or rather gold dust. No need to try to explain
what paying such homage meant to her,
like being in Jane Austen's house in Chawton, England
or Tagore's house in India- at the scene of the...
Not something Tom wanted to do and yet had done.

And their lovemaking here in the English bedroom
of the French chateau was different too,
as if they were a different couple, love-making,
gentle, more careful, more loving, not so sustained.
but long moments lying in each other's arms
or bodies folded into each other's bodies,
sharing this warmth almost a new experience
sharing this warmth an inexorable comfort
but also as if the essence and anger and strength of Tom
was less and less. As then as if he and she were less and less...

Mont Saint-Michele

Not Bayeux though they'd talked of it
but to the fairytale castle, sea-encircled at full moon
with quicksand at low tide-
straight from a children's book, a fairy-tale place,
Mont Saint-Michele.

They read its history as they approached;
built and torn down, then built again
an abbey, a fortress, even a prison at one time,
a monastery of illuminated manuscripts,
1400 years survival now a village
of few hundred folk, and a million tourists,
like them, passing through,
with its sortie of monks and nuns
still extant and still inside the abbey,
so many small shops lining the road upward,
all selling soufflé, savoury or sweet,
all temptingly French. On the way up
they decided on savoury, and he agreed
they were to die for! 'So light! How do they do it?'

She wonders if Charles of the chateau
has a book on his bountiful shelves
that casts light on this magical place.
Did France and England really have a 100 Year War?
The French winning in 1453?
A scramble of names
Henry V and Jean D'arc and all that

Then wonders is it important to know?
Australia, their life so far distant is yet paramount,
It's own dark history defibrillating, compelling,
still more to be told, ingested. Overriding.
Yet this one right here, in its own way, now insisting,
imagining a 100 Year War...

They continue their morning, talking, talking,
their way up and up stairs,
so many flights of them, twists and turns
arched doorways, grand pillars and open spaces,
sudden views of the causeway and retreating tide.
Western terrace they knew had a grand view
'So this must be it?' he said, consulting their map.
Normandy and Brittany both in view either side.
And up and up again to the grand abbey.
Small doorways, glimpses of turrets
everywhere pretty windows but so small
rather meanly set in so much stone,
she said, allowing only slithers of light.
Up more stairs wider and wider
that led into another open space
and he was holding her hand in his
and she liked the warmth of it.

A huge wooden wheel, 'windlass,' authoritative,
'for pulling up goods from way below,' he told her.
'Poor bloody prisoners walked it round and round.
 You know a treadmill - when it was a prison.'

'Terrible,' she agreed.
 She didn't say she'd read the brochure too.

They didn't pause again until the cloisters
with its inner arches housing a garden,
a square of close cut lawn, a jewel green against the stone,
a flagged path to stroll around looking out or not,
meditating, praying, and maybe we should?
Another line, a grand border of more stone arches,
outlining the whole generous space.
Some outer arches filled now with clear glass
and capturing sweeping views.
And Tom choosing to jump up, back against the glass
to pose, spread-eagled and jaunty
as if about to fall back into space
and she sees a momentary Christ figure
in a swirling grey tweed coat,
and calling out to him to come down
but not before a photo he said
and then his leaping down, laughing.
They went on up towards the belltower
hand in hand for the second time
that day.

Sauntering down from the abbey through
the maze of halls and corridors, down steps
through the small town drifting among the crowds
they stop for another soufflé, this time sweet
She is happy.
Today I have been happy, she thinks,
It was so easy. It was pitifully easy.
All the day.

Another of her mother's sent poems…
so soon after to part forever.
But Normandy was, she reached for the words,
something exceptional, and then just simply
Normandy was happy.

Today I have been happy. All the day
I held the memory of you, and wove
Its laughter with the dancing light o' the spray,
And sowed the sky with tiny clouds of love,
And sent you following the white waves of sea,

Maybe it was Tom in his own way,
who loved the pilgrim soul in her
or tried to love the pilgrim soul in her
without knowing or caring about the poem, any poem.
Not Henry and not Rob Connor. Tom?

Tom was drifting away as the water shivered,
as he had but not with spite and anger now!
This was a realisation,
And Evie was able to take comfort
as if in the revisiting, all the hurt, the meanness
and the spite in him was shrunken,
into a small fist ball she could toss away.
Tom exciting and loving and excitable.
Normandy Tom, loving Tom, laughing Tom
let it end here. Exonerated.
Maybe she was finished here at the pond at last.

Totti's story

Staying and thinking its very beginning,
imagining its infant circles...
the careful plotting of garden beds
the considered planting of trees
that assume their places above and below
'That calmly plan to outlive us, lovey!'
as Toby had told her on a tree planting occasion.

The laying out, the looping, hedge-lined paths,
escalating rockeries with their ample plantings.
all such circles over time now raggedly intruded,
hedges gone holey and hay-wire
rockeries bustling with weeds
and faulted rocks gone awry.
Everything falling inwards and downwards
except the most spirited foliage
still clambering up and over
fruiting or flowering again and again despite it all.

'The garden of the world.'
as the old aunt had so wisely called it.
Totti
'Seeds in the earth as basic as that
So much to give...'
Palm leaf displays thrashing in the air
Patterned air, she hears the words,
Patterns moving around us beyond us...
In our making around us.

Thinking on it. Is this lightness Evie asks herself,
the same as brimming?

Brimming.
As if music you have chosen to adore
is imminent or enveloping.
Caresssing weathers, zephyrs, not ordinary breezes
and day colours more than usual,
hanging leaves at a particularly pleasing tilt,
myriads of greens, sage and emerald to khaki,
separating and conjoining, astounding in their greenness,
in their easy display.

Everything, everything coming to a point
so there is a something else risen in you, a lightness?
tantamount to joy.
So that you brim with it
an unreasonable happiness,
love for the world, love for friends
even a new regard for foes...
She couldn't quite manage the word love
when she thought of certain betrayals
 but perhaps in a different regard
seen in this aura if only briefly,
a definitive lightness.

'Gardening lovey, you never tire of it
something new every day, huge changes every season,
something soothing in digging,
dug through a few sorrows of my own.'
And Evie knew Totti was referring to her lost babies
'It's - it's -' and she reached for the word

'Grounding, ha ha!' quite pleased by it.
'Dirt under your nails and roots round your fingers
digging and digging (and things manageable).'
She didn't say the words sorrow manageable
but at last she'd told Evie the story of Samuel
one night when Toby was out,
the story about the crazed death
of her beloved and only brother.

Their problem brother Samuel,
a drinker and a gambler but to excess,
one night over her favourite whisky,
she quietly told it and Evie was glad for it,
given the unburdening the aunt had suffered
so tearfully from her. Samuel.
The brother who'd arrived at their farm gate
incensed all over again by their father's will,
this time gun in hand, 'not for her,' she explained,
'but for Toby!'
To frighten Toby in their farmhouse
given to Totti and Toby by her father,
'Over his own flesh and blood!' Sam had shrieked.

How she'd screamed at Toby not to go out there
where Samuel paced up and down near the gate
under the willow trees at the creek's fertile edge
A slender cat of a man
moving in and out of the willow stripes
gun held loosely in his hand
but obvious for all to see.
His tears and rage, his screaming out,
'You get the farm and I get a pissy town house!

You never gave a bugger about the farm
and the bastard consigns it to you!
To you and Totti
you bloody evil pair!'

'You must have convinced him, the old man
not for me! Not for his spendthrift son.
You must have Toby!
You arsehole, old man cocksucker!
You filth about town with your rich man's hat
these days. Strutting up and down!
Property owner!'

Sobbing in between his mouthfuls,
screaming obscenities so loud
some of the nearby
cows stopped chewing,
looked up from their cud,
surprised for a moment.

And then Toby, No! She's tried to stop him.
But nothing stopping Toby
going out to calm him
as he'd done other times.
and she not far behind.
'But Sam had waited spitefully,'
Totti said with a sigh, spitefully
waited for both of them,
turning the gun on himself as they got close,
so Toby would see full drama of it,
so that she would, too.
'This kind of thing,' she'd said sadly to Evie,

'can change your life it seems forever.
And it did in one way. We had to leave there
where we were so happy.
Leave it all behind us.
But you go on lovey. Like we went on!'

'Dirt under your nails and roots round your fingers
digging and digging, coping with the burden
though never quite uprooting it.'
Sad but not sorry for herself, only for him,
the dead brother.
'I can hold other memories of him, love.'
She offered her outstretched hands
'and I do!' then made two tight fists of them.
'Sam I am,' she laughed. Two tight fists
just as she had for Tom - how amazing!
But then Totti held those two tight fists
close against her heart.

Admission

So many parts revealed, secrets
she was accepting and rejecting
in her own obsessive revisiting
of her short times with Rob Connor
But it was as if she'd been trying to prise some memory
Like Normandy and Tom, that might
in some way release her?

Thinking back on it
the time Rob Connor had been most sincere
was that mountain day she'd shied away from.
He collapsed in her arms after he told her,
crying like a child, could hardly be comforted.
And she could remember, would remember
did remember his confession.
And how in doing so it was the end for them.
His need for her no longer.
And how it might be a kind of ending right now,
to be free of him.

He whispered all the details of it
Of the *murder* as he kept repeating
The murder!
- the way his friend Anton,
had set up the room or had it set up,
the candles, the photos, the paintings,
the books, even the bedcovering,
at the ready. The appointed hour of his visit,

the last exchanges, the embrace, the blemished face
and protuberant eyes of his anguished friend,
poor sad tormented eyes that could no longer cry
though there were cries from his quavering throat,
the bony grabbing hand blotched with dark sores,
that held his. The horror of what he had to do.
The promise had been made.
'I was the only bastard with the courage to do it.
But it has to rest – hardly the word -
on my conscience forever.'
Rob's eyes were welling at this but he went on
'You don't need to...she said.
His last words were thankyou Rob, thankyou!
Oh god! Thankyou. Anton thanking me!
And I murdered him Evie. In cold blood!'

The quivering stopped soon, he died quickly
He had struggled for months
in his lover's house in a foreign place
too ashamed to come home
his beautiful body so marred, his ravaged face,
suffered so much in this graceful room
his life ebbing slowly and then not slowly
for his pernicious incurable shameful illness,
his poor failed body.

And I sat there, and the candles burned down ,
and the big Roman sky outside darkened,
and I remembered he'd warned me, 'get out of here fast'
afterwards, before his partner returned.
But I couldn't leave his poor spent body just yet.
Had to wait for the spirit to leave first...
not saying I saw it, but I felt it all right.

Even said a prayer.
I kissed him, darling Anton, I kissed him and
I looked around that room as if there might be
something of him I could carry with me,
some remnant, some keepsake, something.
I took his leather case, the one he loved
and I knew still carried some of my letters,
as if carrying something of him from that room
completed it. And I left.'

'It changed everything. The world diminished
in front of my eyes, less of everything, you see.
I'd known Anton since school days. Forever really.
He was more than a brother...'

'So now you know,' he was finally calm.
'You know all about me, what I'm capable of.'
This revelation alarming though it was
made him braver than she'd ever thought
but it frightened her too. And the way he repeated,
'I'm a murderer, Evie.' She shivered
the word murderer, bruising, obscene
like an ugly jarring bass note played too loud,
the way he said, 'Murderer!' with such force.
Did he enjoy saying the word, she wondered.
'No Rob!'
'But my friend,' he was surely seeking comfort from her.
She had this picture of him
and his steely resolve to end a life by his own hand.
Thinking of him bending over his friend
ill-prepared, yet prepared to do this.
A mercy killing and yet the image somehow still
alarmed her. She found herself saying,

words of comfort with tears in her eyes.
'He was at death's door.
You helped him through it.
That's all,
A day, an hour earlier.
It was for love of him.'
She took his cold hand in hers
'You were his true friend.'
She was shaking too, as she said it.

Calm now but robbed of
the wholeness of their intimacy,
of their unique mountain sojourn,
the happy parts of it
they found their way back to the village.
She couldn't help noticing on the cold platform
almost empty except for a young girl in a red coat
intent on holding both her boyfriend's hands
as he stared over her head at the tracks,
the sign announcing Katoomba
almost had the word *tomb* as part of it.

She let it all surface now the whole admission
The dreadfulness of his account.
The trembling of his hands afterwards.
The trembling of hers.
Then the brokenness of it, the quiet journey
back to Sydney and themselves.
Something plummeting from its high place.
The restrained parting.
As if an ending announced, quiet, not clashing,
plain sad, perhaps their ending.

Some promise

Why was Rob's story so in-focus just now?
His, a fleeting presence in her youth
and yet prescient. Must have been,
whose appearances, uncommon as they were
surely must explain something?
Why had they been swimming towards her?
and their last day together?

A windy day here, the wind changing everything.
The garden shushes and rustles even scrapes,
a real shuddering creak sometimes from
the unhappy dead frond
lodged in the head of the palm, the wind spookily
making it speak its deliberate language,
if you listened, sometimes obscene. She wouldn't listen.
Obstinate slashes of sunshine were
still changing everything.

Leave the pond but not the garden.
She would reposition by the overgrown pots
Sheltered. Quieter here.
And the wind was dropping on cue.
She would stay and
read the petunias, wonder how
two flowers on the same stem could so differ,
one a pale mauve with deeper purple vein,
one a deep purple with deeper-yet purple veins
radiating outwards from stamens

anther to stigma, to secret reproductive box
as if to find out? Like listening to music
(like Elgar's Nimrod) and almost knowing...

She would look right into the common
nasturtium, vivid yellow with its hairy sheath one side
the calyx of the petals, bursting with yellow pollen too
with its almost perfectly round leaves
veined carefully from a central point, for why?
As if it were in their power
to reveal things to her because she was here, quiet,
quietly looking
The ragged cornflower on its sprawling stem
'Quite overcome,' with tiny pink stamens, a lone ant traversing.
And wait in the sun till the breeze dropped altogether
which it did suddenly, now just a tremble of leaves;
 to help her see into the heart of things...
looking and looking into the heart of things.
There, she'd recalled it, all of it,
something she'd put from her memory
and why, she could wonder,
had it been so difficult?

Was he, Rob Connor, a mirror of her worst self?
Weak, unsure, a fabrication, not quite realised.
Never to be? Yet ostensibly charming and plausible.
Was she dredging him from the past
avoiding most of her life - especially recent trauma,
so that she fled her own shadows with wondering,
ruminating, remembering, going down?
She could hear Totti's and Toby's sensible voices

Chiming together, 'Of course not lovey! Tommy rot,' or
'Utter rubbish,' making her feel steady once more.

'You've got to find lightness again.
That's all pet, and you will.'
Totti's old voice reassuringly said to her
on those occasions when darkness had overtaken.
More frequently now, harder to find lightness,
harder to want to find it. Harder to find light!
Yet she still heard that voice
'You've got to find the lightness in you darling,
And you will Evie, for sure. The light!'
But the thought remained, her worst self?
And what was all this crouching here among the lily pads,
blotches of the past obliterating other memories?

Who she wanted to be
aspiring to be, in Tom-times
even before Tom-times, late adolescence
when everything mattered so fiercely,
everything truly probable, everything likely,
the budding, the promising, poetic, musical,
the fierce need to create, to be wonderful!
Words, ideas budding, spreading, pullulating-
pullulating that word! Horrible sounding word.
But it's right as fecund is too, she mused.

And what of the promise? All the promise?
That thought made her heart knock
 as if there a great weltering weakness resided
even dishonesty, at the centre of it. Her heart,
her vainglorious self, studded as it was

with irresolution, vacillation.
And what else? She wished Totti here to tell her!

All these twirling vines, she thought
looking around her, a mild panic rising, untamed
despite the training and the bending and the clipping
going wild, would pull down the loggia, the house,
longing to hook tendrils in brick and tile,
climb up and up yet pull down. 'And I the princess, under,
100 years hence?' she thought. 'The decaying bones thereof
for I can see holes everywhere, deathly, dark,
in my thinking, in my family, in this very earth.'

'But now I'm looking down
into the pond. And I can make myself
see things more clearly, I'm sure I can.
Rob's story is over for me,' she thought with a definite relief.
'Twice over. All told. Something's over.'

She sat quietly waiting for apprehension to pass,
willing calmness, looking into the depths for it.
And something settled on her like a sable dusk settles,
a slow gentle infiltration of the change of light.

This gorgeous frightening garden,
my friend and not-my-friend
It could move to consume her, she thought,
but will not. No more of this.
It could help her. What, perhaps bloom?
Help her with the struggle
like music does she thought, soothed.

The pond was telling nothing more.
Something was put behind her...
She would write her own words now.
Maybe about Rob, a lot about Tom,
but about others, too.
All right. Try to penetrate that mysterious
group of people bound together
by blood, family, those who'd discarded her
and those she had largely discarded.
Family and round its ragged edges.
The idea made her come alive.

Rob Connor had come to her to complete
a story, hers but not entirely hers, and
she felt strangely happy that he had.
Not just happy, exhilarated!
In the aching light, flickers of that old feeling,
foolish perhaps but inexhaustible.
that there was more to find
more to be had right here
in her house of the decaying interior
and its rampant overgrown exterior,
the garden of the world.
In the dark pond that could,
nonetheless reflect a blueness, like today.
She would like to paint it, to have and to hold it.
She would like to write it, to have and to hold it.
People bound into places bound into her.
Capture more moments she might cherish,
not capture so much as own.
But you cannot 'own' moments
as you cannot 'own' people

(is that the impulse of love 'to *be* the one you love'.)
To somehow ingest the one you love
I am Heathcliff, Don't you see?

But the simple truth is you can't own people,
not even Totti and Toby now that
they were dead. Superbly dead.
The unfussy old-fashioned couple
who'd been there when everyone else...
Family, friends fled or worse, those not to be notified.

The old couple visited her faithfully last time
when she'd been so long at the hospital,
had been the ones who gave her permission
to be herself. To try to be herself. Always there.
Who spoke of ordinary things, not quite knowing
the miracle of those words for her,
who constituted family, in a way
she was sure no one else in the world could.
Despite the gliding psychologists,
regularly in and out of her room,
and the good, eventually calming drugs.
No doubt about those.
And the other kindly spoken counsellors,
and concerned and smiling advisers,
nearly but not quite, almost ready
to go out there once again, they told her.

It was their old voices she heard in the end.
Back to the pond and their voices.
'Come home to us, love,'
Toby and Totti large as life,

seeming to fill the room - Totti in a bright
flowing summer dress she'd made herself
with her too big breasts and plump smooth arms,
pretty and familiar, with her soft lined face,
And Toby, curls slicked into some kind of style
a handsome old man in his best blue shirt,
and favourite not so polished boots,
both of them filling the room
with something hard to explain.
Their good selves as Toby said to friends.
'Just bring your good selves,' when inviting them.

'Come home now,' they said. And she'd gone
with Totti and Toby that very day,
who didn't try to untangle but gave her
a vaulting permission to go on.

Totti's unchanging presence, her largesse,
rooms expanding to her size, seed-in the-earth talks,
and other talks that went over crucially
again and again in her mind as she sought it.
Lightness. Her own.
And Toby's presence beside her.
Unchanging now, his political scepticism.
his growling madness-of-war talks,
his love for a speck of bird life
and his quiet enjoyment of small things;
the slow inhalation of his tobacco in a favourite pipe,
the small bird's cadences and other outside birds,
the Saturday table and wonders of the racing form,
the way he called Totti love and her, lovey...
and the safety of them, just being with them.

The unsurpassable safety. A gift to her, for her.

'Other interests darling. Watch out for them.
Look, you could follow the horsies with us? Nah- not you, is it?'
Totti brightened, 'I took up tap-dancing once you know'
It made her laugh out loud at the very thought of Totti tapping.
They both laughed so hard Toby called out,
'What's so funny?' making them laugh even more.
Totti tapping and she Evie tapping alongside. Safe again.

Someone had once told her about this feeling.
It was something to do with your actual nervous system,
the feeling of safety. Vagus nerve stuff.
Some biological fulfilment?
Simple as that, a strong survival instinct. But more.
Something unknown, yearned for, and somehow fulfilled.
What was yearned for? How fulfilled?
Something elemental then.
'Breathe on me breath of life'
that ridiculous splinter of light
ragged impish hope almost in reach.
Why did it come every time
scruffy and rag tag
yet persistent, to tease,
to impart, to lure, to awkwardly
begin the mend?
Here in the garden of the world.
Evie looked around her slowly, deliberately now.

Every palm and epiphyte, ginger plant and bird of paradise,
those canna lilies, that hibiscus and escaped bougainvillea,
she was in the garden of the world!

Every leaf, every twig, every bird and bush,
every weed, every struggling vine, every gust of flowers,
every speckled, stippled leaf clump,
every delicate network of awesome spiderweb,
the very ground beneath her, leaf littered and aromatic
studied deliberately
so that she knew for more than a moment in time
she was in love with it. All of it.
The garden of the world,
her garden, in her city, Sydney, at the same time.

Evie rose from damp ground,
determined somehow,
with new strength it seemed,
some new spiritual fortitude,
almost like moving on into the future
more protected now, sheltered.
In some inexplicable way it had dawned on her
that there were still moments to gaze
in dark mirrors and see light reflected after all.
Totti and Toby's voices, their sheltering house,
their sheltering garden, and overgrown pathways,
her house now, her garden now. Her world.

Enough now she decided. Epic understanding.
Maybe even reach out to that phantom family
the long-lost brother, a long ago cousin
search the mostly unread letters of the dead mother
packaged carefully somewhere in this house
in some new to-be-discovered way,
whether or not, she would do it,
The very pleasure of rooms she would find

all of them her own
and yet redolent with those she loved
and who had loved her.

A lightness, an agility? she thought and smiled at this
and yet as she walked up the garden path
leaving the peerless pond behind her,
she couldn't help but shiver a little at her going,
even though the sun was shining
and evening shadows were still far off.

finis

Acknowledgement

With her formidable experience in books and publishing, I wish to thank Debbie Lee, head of Ginninderra Press, for support and guidance with this verse novel. It is a work written over some seven years and I feel fortunate indeed to have found such a publisher and such a publishing house. Ginninderra means throwing out rays of light, and Debbie has been a guiding light from ready advice and scrupulous editing to just-the-right cover choice. But it is her enthusiasm for poetry and its power (in keeping with the late Stephen Matthews, former publisher) that is most inspiring to me - and a belief which I share, that the world is still in need of it.

Fragments of poetry

Lawrence Durrell, *This Unimportant Morning*
John Keats, *Ode to a Nightingale* and *To Autumn*
Dylan Thomas, *The Force That Through the Green Fuse Drives the Flower*
Rainer Maria Rilke, *Duino Elegies*
Rupert Brooke, *These I have loved* and *All day I have been happy*
Rubaiyat of Omar Khayyam, Fitzgerald translation
Henry Kendall, *Bellbirds*
Yevgeny Yevtushenko, *Colours.*
William Shakespeare from A *Midsummer Night's Dream*
Banjo Paterson, *The Man from Snowy River*

Poems

Libby Hathorn, *Nui Dat Australian Task Force Headquarters,* Vietnam Reflections (Pax Press, 2012)
Spiderweb
I felt the dread
State Theatre Foyer, a Memory, Shining City Sydney (Pacific Ocean Press, 2025)

Libby Hathorn is a celebrated Australian author, poet and librettist whose work has touched generations of readers in Australia and beyond. Her stories have been translated and adapted for stage, screen and opera. Libby is known for blending lyrical storytelling with social themes winning numerous awards for her work. Poetry has always been an overarching influence in her writing and in her life.

libbyhathorn.com